I0666369

TOP HATS
&
JOCKSTRAPS

First Edition

Published by The Nazca Plains Corporation
Las Vegas, Nevada
2007

ISBN: 978-1-934625-41-5

Published by

The Nazca Plains Corporation ®
4640 Paradise Rd, Suite 141
Las Vegas NV 89109-8000

PUBLISHER'S NOTE
Top Hats & JockStraps is a work of fiction created wholly by *Dutch Roberts'* imagination.   All characters are fictional and any resemblance to any persons living or deceased is purely by accident. No portion of this book reflects any real person or events.

Cover, Dutch Roberts
Art Director, Blake Stephens

Dedication

For all the noble fellowships I have formed along the way.
And, for all the men who have succeeded at work *and* at play.

Acknowledgement

This collection would still be sitting on the electronic boards of a website, viewed only by a select few, if it were not for the existence of one man – Mr. Christopher Trevor. So, with sincere appreciation and utmost gratitude, I must tip my hat to you, Sir.

As to the members of my dear fellowship - accolades, one and all, for your unwavering love and support. You bow to no one.

TOP HATS
&
JOCKSTRAPS

First Edition

Dutch Roberts
Edited by Christopher Trevor

Contents

Richie (This Doesn't Make Sense)
by Christopher Trevor

Man, what a hot fucking trip this was; what a great fucking way to spend lunch hour. I was wearing Richie's shoes, the sexy slip-on ones he always left under his locker before changing to his grungy work boots when he would get to work. Don't know why, but the handsome dark eyed fuck always wore his black slip-on dress shoes to work and then changed to his boots when he got there. And those shoes fit me as well, all this couldn't be more perfect let me tell you bud. And thin navy blue dress socks, Richie always wore those sexy damn navy blue dress socks, never thick white sweat socks like the rest of us factory worker's wore. I guessed Richie thought he was sophisticated or something. At the moment I was very busy, *very* fucking busy actually, squatting behind him and licking and sucking and slurping Richie's big bulging balls. They were tied off at the base of his big juicy cock and yanked down as far as possible behind and under his sexy ass crack with the slack of the rope I had wound securely on them. He grunted, gasped, gurgled and heaved breathlessly and angrily as my tongue slathered greedily over his big stinking balls. His sac was sexy and hairless, his balls were the size of two ping-pong balls and they were funky and delicious beyond any explanation I could give you. The rest of the guy smelled like he had showered that morning, but like the majority of guys out there his balls absolutely stunk. There wasn't all that much the guy could do to stop me eating his balls either, as his big muscular arms were tied tightly at the biceps and cinched up somewhat painfully behind him *and* he was blindfolded. The rope around Richie's biceps extended downward and was tied off to the slack of rope that I had wound around the base of his sexy balls. Fucking handsome guy didn't have a goddamned clue as to who it was that had him in this fucked up position, (fucked up for him great for me) eating his balls and in the company locker room no less...

Richie was wearing just his white sweaty tee shirt rolled up over his nipples and his navy blue dress socks pushed down around his calves as I licked and slathered my tongue over and over and over his mangy balls. Each time I pulled on the rope wound around them and slurped them as far into my mouth as possible the guy grunted loudly in a mixture of pain and ecstasy and pulled himself to his sexy toes. His long sexy toes were outlined beautifully in his thin sweaty navy blue socks. He gyrated his muscular and well-toned body helplessly and involuntarily as I sucked his balls heartily, applying pressure to them with my tongue. The poor fuck was sweating at that point and stinking with it, all signs of his morning shower having disappeared, but fuck it, I had no intention of stopping, at least not until lunch hour was over bud. Fuck, fuck, I had dreamed of this since meeting Richie, when we had hired the twenty-six year old guy with the handsome face akin to that of Prince Charming. I had heard it said via rumors that that was what some of the guys in the factory called Richie, Prince Charming. I pressed the guy up against his closed locker and spread his smooth delectable ass cheeks apart, baring his rosebud. Richie's pink ass hole stared at me, twitching actually, begging for some attention. I didn't hesitate. I plunged my tongue into his sexy stink hole and flicked it around in there, sending chills through the guy. He nearly jumped out of his damned sexy navy blue socks and he trembled like crazy as I now sucked the walls of his mangy stink hole.

"*Fuck,* this doesn't make sense," Richie whispered and balled his meaty dangling hands into fists.

Those were the only words he had spoken since finding himself in this fucked up position... (As stated, fucked up for him, great for me...)

I held his velvety feeling smooth ass cheeks apart and helped myself to generous servings of eating and eating his stink hole, drooling in there uncontrollably and slurping it up in heat. Richie pressed his hard cock against his locker and began rubbing it there. The fact that his cock was hard attested to the fact that somehow, somewhere deep inside him perhaps, the Prince Charming handsome guy was enjoying this... But not yet I thought and used the rope around his balls to yank his cock back and under his sexy ass crack. He grunted and heaved angrily again as I stopped eating his hole and slurped again at those stinking balls of his that I had fallen so damned hard for...

"No, this doesn't make sense," Richie repeated.

Richie is Spanish, from Ecuador to be exact. He has dark sad looking sexy piercing eyes, black silky hair cut short and neatly combed to the side like a young boy would do. His body is muscular and very, very well toned from the work that we do in the factory and from working out at the gym as well and he is as smooth as a baby all over his body, save for the hair on his head, his pubic bush and armpits. So many times I had seen him standing there changing clothes in the locker room. So many times I saw the guy stripped to his white briefs and those sexy navy blue dress socks he wears. The bulge in his briefs always left me breathless. Even from the few lockers away that I am from him I could see those two big balls bulging and outlined erotically in his briefs. One time he stood there nonchalantly having a conversation with one of the other workers while wearing just his briefs and socks. There was definitely something erotic about that. I mean, Richie standing there in just his briefs and socks and having a conversation with a guy who was fully clothed. It told me that Richie had the utmost confidence in himself that's for sure. Each time he scratched those big balls of his my breath caught in my throat. I knew that somehow I just had to get my mouth wrapped around those big juicy balls of his. What a waste they were just sitting in the pouch of his briefs. But how, that was the problem. Most times after changing into our work gear we find that we are assigned to work in buildings and lots that are a train ride away from our home base or in factories that are away from our home base. On this day however we had the luck of being assigned to a building that was just two blocks from our home base. That meant we didn't have to spend carfare and we could even have lunch in our lunchroom. The lunchroom is connected to our locker room, which is where I got the snag on Richie and ate his balls till he couldn't stand it and till they were more than good, engorged and swollen.

Holding the slack of rope in my hand I pulled on it a little and brought Richie's big thick veined cock head further out from under his ass crack. I snickered as some of my saliva dripped out of his beautiful and stinky ass crack. Fuck, I had really done a job sopping up his hole let me tell you. Richie again almost flew out of his socks, this time because I had wrapped my lips around his thick throbbing shaft. Richie's cock is easily eight to nine inches long, fat and as I said, thickly veined. A real treat for a cock hungry fucker like me let me tell you. I loved sucking his monster-sized cock, but it was those balls of his that had me totally mesmerized. He involuntarily bent himself slightly over as I greedily slid his cock further into my mouth. He gasped and panted loudly as I sucked him and sucked him like crazy, holding that rope taut in my hand, forcing his cock and balls to stay where they were, just under his smelly, funky and moist ass crack.

"Fuck man, this doesn't make sense at all," Richie said breathlessly.

Poor fucking guy was in this position only because he had decided to have lunch in the locker room instead of sitting in the lunchroom with the other guys from the crew that day. I had gone into the locker room to get some money from my locker when I saw Richie sitting in a chair by his locker. He had finished eating and a paper back book was on the floor at his feet. He was sitting there fast asleep. I guessed that the morning work in that office building had really tired the guy out. I figured that he had brought the chair into the locker room so that he could eat by himself and then do some reading. Grinning fiendishly, I thought how that would become his undoing. I silently made my way over to him, realizing also that we were the only two guys in the musty scented locker room at that moment and would be for the rest of our lunch break. He was sitting there with his head hanging back, his mouth partly open and breathing evenly. He was definitely asleep, not just dozing. Fuck, just looking at him took my breath away and caused my cock to grow hard and erect in my jeans. I cautiously knelt in front of the sleeping prince and sniffed the crotch of his jeans. His balls were outlined beautifully there. His crotch smelled musty and sweaty, like he had been working all morning. I picked up his empty soda bottle and sniffed the top of it. Richie's lips scent was still on it and that sent a shiver of delight through me. I stood up and leaned down over the guy, my nose close to his slightly parted lips. I sniffed his lips and wanted desperately to kiss him. (Fuck, I could have kissed the sleeping prince a thousand times over and over...) But I knew that he couldn't know it was I. Fucking guy is the biggest goddamned skirt chaser on our crew. And I have seen how the women look at and ogle Richie when we work outdoors. When the weather is hot he purposely takes off his tee shirt, knowing that it drives the women passerby crazy to see him with his massively muscular chest bared. Without thinking I took my long red bandanna out of my back pocket. If he woke up while I was doing this I would simply say that I had been planning to play a joke on him. Someone up there was on my side because he didn't even stir as I tied my sweaty bandanna over his eyes, blindfolding him. Fuck, he looked even sexier now with his eyes covered. It gave him something like an air of mystery. I was halfway there to getting my mouth wrapped around those big sweaty and bulging balls of his. I looked down at the floor and saw what was leftover of a pack of packaging rope near Richie's locker. I looked up at the ceiling and silently asked God if he was trying to tell me something. I picked up the heavy-duty rope and began carefully winding it around and around one of Richie's big biceps. His arms were dangling down at the sides of the chair, making it easy for me to get his arms roped up. There was no turning back now. He stirred slightly in the chair as I tied the rope around his first arm. With my heart pounding like crazy I pulled his other arm close to the tied one and quickly began tying that one as well, winding the rope securely around it. It was at that point that Richie woke up. As he tried to stand up he was still kind of groggy I pulled the rope taut, yanking his bound arms painfully behind him. I quickly and efficiently tied the ends of the ropes together, cinching his biceps upwards behind him.

"Uhhhhffff???" Richie gasped, trying to take in his present situation.

Being blindfolded made it a little more than difficult for the poor prince of a guy, as he could not get his bearings. I moved back in front of him and slowly unlaced his grungy work boots. He squirmed in the chair as I slid his smelly boots off his feet. I heartily sniffed the inside of each of them.

"Wha," Richie began to say but when he felt my hands on his socked feet he leaned back in the chair and grimaced miserably.

I caressed his navy blue socked feet and sniffed one of them with total gusto. For a pair of dress socks they sure smelled pretty rancid I thought. Smiling meanly I helped the guy to his socked feet by holding his tied biceps real fucking tight and undid his jeans. A look of horror seemed to come over Richie's blindfolded face as I slid his jeans down and off him.

"H-hey, this doesn't make sense," Richie said, sounding totally confused but not all that scared.

After getting his jeans off him I knelt in front of him, grabbed his muscular thighs from the back and pressed my face against his crotch, the prize that I had sought all this time. I breathed in the scent of the construction prince's underpants and I swear I fell in love with him then and there. Richie's briefs were moist and scented with man sweat and a small lingering odor of piss was on them as well. I pressed my lips against his outlined balls in the briefs and kissed them hard a few times.

"God, I love your balls Richie," I whispered, not wanting him to know who it was that was having their way with him.

His mouth dropped open in shock as I moved my mouth, my tongue and my lips all over his sweaty scented briefs. I moved my hands down to his navy blue socks and pushed them down to his calves. He sure looked all sexy and helpless let me tell you. But not once did he call out for help. After a few minutes I hooked my thumbs in the sides of his briefs and in a quick pull I had them off him. I stood up and stuffed his briefs into my back jeans pocket. I rolled Richie's tee shirt up till his big brown fleshy nipples were visible for my use. He grimaced but didn't say a word as I gave his nipples a hard squeeze and twist each. Holding his hot nips between my thumbs and first two fingers of each hand I pulled Richie forward. He took a few awkward steps on his socked feet and his cock grew fear hard in front of him. Obviously the prince had very sensitive nips. It was at that point that I spied those slip-on shoes of his under his locker. Smiling, I guided him over to the locker next to his, propped him up against it and leaned in real close to him, my lips just about grazing his trembling ones.

"Th-*this doesn't make sense,*" he said softly through his trembling lips.

"Don't make any noise and you'll be fine," I whispered to him and gently kissed his lips.

As he stood there taking deep panicky sounding breaths I got my work boots off and slipped those shoes of his onto my sweat-socked feet. A feeling of out-right kink consumed me as I slid Richie's shoes onto my feet.

"Now for those balls of yours," I whispered and took the guy by his bound arms.

Richie grimaced again behind his blindfold as I turned him around facing the lockers. I knelt behind him, grabbed his sac and yanked it toward me between his sexy and creamy thighs. He stood there trembling in his socks with his muscular legs parted as I tied a good length of rope around his balls, just under his cock. I pulled the rope tight and he let out a pain filled sounding gasp. With the slack of the rope held in my hand I held his big smelly balls under his equally smelly ass crack and greedily began licking the fuck out of them.

"Ohhhhhhhh," Richie moaned and looked straight up.

And so for fifteen minutes into our lunch hour I sucked, licked and slurped heartily on the guy's big balls. His muscles strained mightily and flexed involuntarily in his arms as he tried in vain to get himself untied. But it was no use. I had tied him too tight. He was mine for the moment, totally mine. I thought of all those women checking him out as he worked bare chested and a feeling of total kink again coursed through me. His hands clenched into angry meaty fists dangled uselessly at his sides...

As I sucked his cock I knew the guy was getting close to shooting his load. I could feel his meat stick throbbing like crazy in my mouth. It would be the first load that I got out of him during that lunch break...

Richie panted in ecstasy and I quickly took his cock out of my mouth. I held it in my hand under his ass crack and it erupted in a jet stream of jizz.

"Ohhhhhhhh, ohhhhhhhh, th-this doesn't make sense," Richie grunted as I stroked his spewing cock, his jizz landing on the floor a few feet from where I had him standing.

He danced sexily and stupidly on his socked feet, swiveling his delectable ass cheeks as I stroked every last drop out of the handsome prince of a guy. When he was done and trying to catch his breath I let go of his cock, grabbed the slack of the rope around his cock and balls and yanked it hard, bringing those big balls of his close for more torture. Richie again gasped in pain as I yanked his balls back and then slid my tongue all over them.

"Ayyyyyyy, no, this doesn't make sense," Richie repeated again as I pursed my lips around his balls and sucked hard.

Richie heaved and grunted miserably. No doubt, like most other guys out there, his balls were feeling real sensitive after just having shot that load. I stopped sucking his balls after a few minutes, ran my tongue up and down those exquisite ass cheeks of his more than a few times and then spread them apart. His bung hole stared at me all sweaty and stinky. I plunged my tongue into his hole for another good go at it. Richie grunted, pulled himself to his toes and swiveled himself like a sexy dancer of sorts. As I licked one of his smooth ass cheeks I gave the other one a good hard slap or two.

"Ouuucchhh!!!" Richie seethed. "Fuck, this doesn't make sense..."

A half-hour had gone by and by then Richie's balls were pretty sore and swollen looking as I had spent the better part of that half-hour really working them big-time. To give his balls a break I propped the guy against his locker (facing forward) and slurped one of his big brown fleshy nipples into my mouth. Some break huh? First I worked the fuck out of his balls, now it was his nipples turns. I nipped hard at his nipple with my front teeth, licked and sucked the fuck out of the nub and even kissed it a few times as well. Richie's cock was hard, dribbling pre cum and pointing straight out in front of him as I worked the fuck out of his nipple. With my fingers I squeezed and teased his other nipple. Sweat dripped down the guy's muscular smooth chest and he grimaced miserably every time I bit hard on his nipple. He was starting to smell as funky as the locker room itself.

"Now, let's see," I whispered, took my fingers off his nipple and reached down to grab his hard cock.

I stroked the muscled prince a few times and he spewed a second load of Ecuadorian jizz nearly all the way across the locker room.

"Ayyyyrrrrrrr!!!!" the guy seethed in the forced ecstasy as I sucked his nipple meanly and stroked his cock like crazy. "Uhhhhhrrrr, m-makes no sense..."

Richie again pulled himself to his socked toes, swiveled his hips like an exotic dancer and sprayed jets of cum from his wide and sexy slit. He grunted, heaved and was sweating profusely by then. When he was done shooting his load the second time I stopped working his nipple and let go of his cock. He lowered himself to his feet and hung his head down.

"Th-this doesn't make sense," he whispered as I picked up another good length of rope.

We still had more than twenty minutes of lunchtime left and I didn't plan to waste a second of them...

A few minutes later I had Richie standing in front of his locker facing forward. The slack of the rope tied around his cock and balls was now pulled under him and the end of it tied off to the hasp of his combination lock. He stood there docile and helpless with his balls tucked under his smelly ass crack as I knelt in front of him, sucking the fuck out of his cock. The guy grimaced and clenched his teeth in a mixture of ecstasy and agony as I sucked, scraped and really worked his big over-sized sausage like crazy. He had already shot two hefty loads for me and I knew that he was having no problem cooking up a third batch of his good stuff in those balls of his for me. With the rope pulled taut around his balls and tied to his lock hasp he had no choice but to stand there utterly frozen. He grunted and his huge chest heaved out nice and big as I suckled just the very tip of his sexy cock, really driving him crazier than crazy. I poked my tongue into his slit and that nearly sent the prince flying out of his socks and through the ceiling. He arched his back and forced his cock deep into my mouth. As the guy said over and over, this was making no sense to him, still the way he suddenly fucked my throat showed me how much he was secretly enjoying the trip I had taken him on. I grabbed his thighs from behind and pulled him further into my warm mouth and even further down my throat. Fucking handsome prince loved this shit there no goddamned denying it at that point. Richie's body broke out in goose bumps, as he stood there arched and gasping, getting close to shooting that third load.

"Ohhhhhhhhhhhh, ma-makes no sense," Richie blubbered and then shot his third load, right into my mouth. "Ohhhhhhhhh!!!!!"

His Ecuadorian jizz tasted like magic. I gulped him down madly, sucking his cock at the same time, really making him crazy at that point.

"Ohhhhhhhhhhhh!!!!" the guy grunted as the last spurts of jizz erupted from his huge cock.

When he was done again I let his cock slip slowly from my mouth, smacking my lips together in delight I reached under the guy and gave his sensitive balls a gentle squeeze, sort of saying thank you I suppose. Then, I stood up and knew that I had to get out of there. I also had to untie the guy so that no one would find him in the position that he was presently in. But at the same time I could not have him seeing me. As he stood there catching his breath I slipped Richie's shoes off my feet, placed them back under his locker and quickly got my boots back on.

"Th-this doesn't make sense," Richie whispered, listening as I got my boots on.

Now I had to be very fast, *very fast indeed.* I quickly kissed the prince's lips and reached behind him. I loosened the ropes around his biceps just a little, affording me enough time to get out of the locker room before he got himself completely loose and took off the blindfold. As Richie began to struggle out of the loosened ropes I dashed quietly out of the locker room. I heard Richie say, "This doesn't make sense" as he got himself slowly untied. By the time he got the blindfold off I was long gone...

About ten minutes later there was a knock on my office door, the door with the word "Foreman" on it.

"Come in," I called out, sitting behind my desk.

Richie came in looking more than tired.

"Mr. Devlin?" Richie asked as he came over to my desk.

"Yes Richie, what can I do for you?" I asked the handsome guy, noticing that he was wearing his slip-on black shoes.

"I-I think I'm going to go home for the rest of the day, if that's okay with you Sir," he said, sounding very exhausted. "I'm really kind of beat from the heat out there today and it doesn't make sense, but I'm not feeling right."

"Okay Richie, go on home, I'll have Reggie cover you for the rest of your shift," I said to him, sounding sympathetic. "Feel better okay?"

"Yeah, thanks Sir," he said and turned his back.

As he walked out of my office I saw my red bandanna sticking out of his back pocket. I smiled and reached into my back pocket. I pulled out Richie's stinking briefs and sniffed them heavily...

Foreword from the Editor

I always wondered if the above story would find a place somewhere. When I wrote it I wondered if other guys out there had a fetish for wearing other guy's clothing. Until this book and until I met the author I did not realize the fetish was so prevalent. As was stated by the author of "Twisted Tales from the Tank", Steve Geary, "With the right mix every hidden desire and emotion can surface. There are fascinating mysteries within all of us, and combining them with sex multiplies the thrill a thousand fold." And so I found with newcomer author, "Dutch Roberts." The man embodies all the elements of a suave, dapper tuxedo wearing gentleman on a Saturday evening performance of a ballet or opening of a Broadway show. He personifies the look of a stern, masculine yet sexy Wall Street executive in a business suit. But as dapper and as elegant as these two looks are he also knows the sleazy and grubby joys of a sweaty construction worker in worn jeans, a sweat sopped tee shirt and stinking moist thick socks along with clonky mustard colored work boots. He knows the thrills of a convict who manages to suit himself up in a rich man's clothing when said convict manages to weasel his way into the man's home when no one is there. He knows the joys of how a young man feels when he puts on his first designer suit...along with all the spiffy gear that goes along with it. Yes, Mr. Dutch Roberts knows the joys of all those looks and swapping them between the characters he creates. Having the assailant in my above story "Richie (This Doesn't Make Sense")" wear the bound guy's shoes while working him over has now become a definite homage to Mr. Dutch Roberts. When I first put out my "Call for Submissions" for writers to send me their work for future books Mr. Dutch Roberts was the first gentleman to reply. I read his first two stories "Phantom" and "Bait and Switch" and was instantly hooked. Whereas I had had a guy wearing another guy's shoes in my intro story for his book, Dutch Roberts has his characters totally switch identities in some sections. He expertly mixes the two contrasts wonderfully, the suave well-dressed gentleman and the sweaty musty scented construction worker at the end of a long hot grueling day.

The setting for "Phantom" could not be better, a private box in a theater during a riveting performance of a Broadway show perhaps, a real-life phantom mysteriously appearing to the gentleman who occupies the box, and a fantasy played out that so many of us have only thought about...

"Bait and Switch" combines the elements of contrast between sleazy leather men in denim gear and well-dressed tuxedo clad gentlemen along with a kinky ambush in a leather bar, such as Timmy Backman encountered in "Timmy at the Leather Bar", but these guys are just a touch more aggressive when it comes to their well-dressed adversaries.

And those are just two of the stories that await readers with this unique fetish in this book...

I am honored and pleased to bring to you the works and talent of "Mr. Dutch Roberts."
-Christopher Trevor-

Foreword from the Author

Oh man, do I have a four letter word for you and it starts with the letter f.

Wanna hear it?

Ok. Here goes...

Fate.

Now, for those of you who thought I was going to say "fuck," well, sit tight, you nasty little pigs, the fucking comes later on. To those of you who didn't – more power to you. We appear to be on the same page...for now. To be honest, I plan on getting into the fucking that the others were just thinking about, however, let's take a moment to discuss a little thing known as fate.

Over the last few years I have discovered that fate does indeed play a major role in our lives. It can work *for* us or, regretfully at times, *against* us. It can appear in mysterious ways or it can slide right in, crystal clear, from the very first moment. Believe it or not, take it or leave it, it's there.

In the case of *Top Hats & Jockstraps*, fate washed over me like the first few sparkling drops of jizz from a jocks throbbing, fully erect cock. You know what I'm talking about. You've seen it first hand. Right before a hot stud is ready to explode, there is that delicious, bubbling stream of pre seed and it is *always* crystal clear.

Until recently, I was simply sharing my work, for free, on a wonderful site. The site, from the start was a dream come true for a man such as me. It beautifully catered to my every desire and passion in regard to my fetish for both suits and, in particular, formal wear. There, on my computer screen, time and time again, I was treated to an exquisite feast of beautiful images and movies. Each update seemed to be formulated just for me, as if someone – or something – was reading my mind.

My secret fetish, which was rather new and rarely explored at the time, was suddenly coming to life right before my very eyes. However, what was more startling was the fact that there were others out there who felt as I did. Clearly, Matt & Rico – the men who created the site – shared a love for the subject matter, but now I was interacting with a world of men who could appreciate the look and feel of a beautifully tailored suit. There were others, beside myself, who had the desire to "play" in such garments.

In the blink of an eye I quickly began to realize that I was not alone.

As the years flowed by, I soon began to dabble in writing erotic fiction based on this classy fetish. Before long, I was crafting fantastical stories around conversations I had had with other members. Along the way, we would also exchange information we had in regard to fetish related sites or groups – several of which I joined right away.

My body of work continued to evolve and grow as the site and the number of members did. I began to branch out, exploring the many different angles of the suit fetish world. Soon, I found myself not only adding twists to my work, but also to my sex life. I firmly believed then, as I do now, that you can only sing one note for so long. Sooner or later your voice will give out. So, the more I was exposed to, the more I embraced the subtle changes that were occurring within me, as well as to my original fetish.

At one time, I simply enjoyed going through the motions of shopping for a new suit or tuxedo. I took great pleasure in selecting the items, trying them on, and then wearing them out and about. These steps were a subtle form of foreplay to me. The feeling of it was like nothing else in the world. Then, I found myself bringing these garments into the bedroom. Soon, suited sex was a part of my life. However, in time, after speaking to many different members of the site, I discovered that I could integrate a little foot play, or bondage, or clothes swapping, and still maintain the enjoyment of the suit or tuxedo. As these changes took place in my real life they began to also slip more and more into the fictional worlds I created.

Then, the moment came for fate to toss me a bone. Or should I say boner?

Having joined several suit related groups over the years, I currently receive numerous emails with notices or updates pertaining to the happenings of these groups. Sometimes it can be nothing more than a hot photo of a suited stud; however, one particular email contained a call for erotic submissions by celebrated author Christopher Trevor.

Figuring that I had nothing to lose, I drafted up an email and sent one of my short stories to Mr. Trevor. Immediately, to my surprise, I received a reply – a *very* positive reply. Once we connected and began speaking on the phone, we soon realized that we were clearly cut from the same cloth. Our ability to see the many dimensions of a fetish ran parallel to one another. Our views on how we expressed our desires were also a mirror image. It was like finding a long lost friend, perhaps even a soul mate of sorts, one who could easily finish a sentence or a thought without hesitation. I firmly believe that fate brought us together, one step at a time, and I am truly thankful for that. I couldn't have asked for a better editor, mentor, and friend for my first time as a published writer.

So, without further ado, it's time to suit up, sit back, and enjoy the erotic ride that is *Top Hats & Jockstraps*. Join me in "Phantom", as we bear witness to a passionate evening at the opera where men in suits and formal wear explore each other for the first time in the privacy of their box seat. However, the pleasures certainly don't end with the last curtain call. In "Bait and Switch" we find ourselves still suited to the nines but suddenly on the wrong side of the tracks, so to speak. In a seedy leather bar two very different worlds collide and the outcome is rather surprising, but completely rewarding. In "Paying Dues" we join a young man as he discovers how it feels to live the high life after he acquires-with the help of a strapping officer of the law-his first designer suit. "Quartet" places us in that big, red, leather swivel chair, down at the local barber shop where a cut and shave will leave you longing for your next appointment and a shoe shine-in the tradition of Christopher Trevor-will leave your feet, as well as your loins burning for another rub. "Torn" leads us into one man's dark fantasy where a single move can alter his reality forever. "Riches to Rags" takes us on a dangerous romp through a wealthy estate where every desire and whim can be played out-for a price. However, "TJ" swiftly brings us back to the real world, in an all-too familiar setting of a locker room, where an obsessed fan is discovered by the very object of his desire.

Are you ready?

I thought so.

Let the hot, steamy, formal fucking begin.

Dutch Roberts

2007

Phantom

As Colin sat in the taxicab, racing toward the Metropolitan Opera House, he began to realize just how much he hated evenings such as this. His fiancée always attempted to make it sound like fun, but in reality, he always found it to be very boring. He wasn't sure why he gave in so easily. If he had the balls, he would have made the driver turn right around and take him home, but he knew that she would be waiting for him on the steps to the performance hall. He couldn't just leave her there waiting. Could he?

"Driver, this will do," Colin called, as they approached the hall.

"Yes Sir," the driver replied, as he pulled the vehicle toward the curb.

"Here, keep the change," Colin noted, as he handed the driver several bills from his leather wallet.

"Thank you, Sir. Enjoy the performance," the driver replied, as he reset the meter to zero.

"Hmm, I'm not too sure about that," Colin muttered, as he slid out of the cab, grabbing his hat along the way.

Standing now, at the base of the performance hall courtyard, Colin watched as eager patrons rushed up the steps to make the opening act. He found it somewhat amazing that anyone would actually want to hurry to such a dreadful event.

"Colin! Over here," he suddenly heard, just to the right of where he was standing.

Looking up, in the general direction of the call, he saw his fiancée waving franticly, attempting to get his attention.

"I see you. I see you. There's no need to wave me down," Colin commented, as he approached her.

"I thought you were going to wear your tuxedo tonight," she replied with a pout on her rosebud lips, as she leaned in to kiss him on his clean-shaven cheek.

"No. I never said that. You know how much I hate the way I look in it. It's just too damn formal and restrictive for my taste. I feel more comfortable in a suit," Colin snapped back, as he adjusted his pale, silver-grey, silk tie.

"Oh, and a three-piece pinstripe isn't restraining?" she jokingly mocked him in return.

"For me? No. Can we head inside now? I think I may need a drink before the performance," Colin noted, as he took her by the arm, escorting her up the steps.

"You know I hate it when you drink," she whispered, as they passed through the main doors of the performance hall.

"That's not what you said the other night," Colin replied with a devilish grin on his lips.

"Well, it does bring out the bad boy in you," she toyed back with a slight smile on her lips.

"Why don't you head inside? I'll meet you upstairs," Colin directed, as he made his way for the lobby bar.

"Oh, sure, just don't take too long," she replied, as she passed through the interior doors, heading up the steps toward the private box that her family reserved and shared for the season.

Free of her, Colin strode toward the bar eager to down a few smooth ones before the performance. It seemed, from the line, he wasn't the only one who needed to prepare for the ever-so-riveting evening. Standing just off to the side, he glanced around the room. Oddly, he found himself watching the men in particular. His eyes were drawn to the formally attired gentlemen who seemed to be decked out above and beyond what was truly needed for such a performance.

"Penguins," Colin muttered.

"Excuse me?" a man standing to his left replied.

"Nothing. Ignore me," Colin replied, as he caught the profile of the man in his view.

"I'm pretty sure you just called the formal men of this room... penguins," the man continued.

"Yeah, so, what if I did?" Colin barked back, suddenly realizing, as he turned to face him, that the man was also dressed in a tuxedo.

"That's pretty funny," the man replied, with a huge smile on his handsome face.

"Sorry. I didn't mean...," Colin mumbled now, attempting to save face.

"No. It's fine. No offense taken. The name is Antonio. May I buy you a drink?" the man replied, as he put out a hand to shake.

"Uh, Colin, and sure, as long as I can buy you one in return during the intermission," he replied with a smirk on his face and a firm handshake.

"Well, nice to meet you Colin and, might I add, you look rather sharp in your choice of suits tonight," Antonio commented, as he gave Colin the once over.

"Oh, this old thing, I've had it for years," he replied, as he ran a hand over the dark blue suit, with its faint white pinstripes.

"Well, it suits you well," Antonio noted in return, with a smile on his lips, before placing their drink order with the bartender.

Colin moved away from the bar now, suddenly feeling somewhat awkward. He couldn't help but wonder if this guy was hitting on him. It wasn't like this would be the first time that this had happened, but, for some reason he found this guy and his advances a bit too forward. Fumbling with his hat, in his now slightly damp hands, he watched as the impeccably dressed man approached him with their drinks.

"Here," Antonio prompted Colin.

"Thank you," Colin replied, as he took the drink, fighting the desire to decline it now.

"So, did you come alone this evening?" Antonio boldly questioned, as he sipped his drink.

"No, actually, I'm here with my fiancée," Colin replied a bit too abruptly.

"Ah, well, enjoy the performance with her. I hear that it is supposed to be a rather erotic one," Antonio replied in return, as he finished his drink. "I guess I will see you at the intermission."

"Uh, sure, for that drink...right?" Colin stammered, as he downed the rest of his current drink.

"Correct. You didn't think I was going to let you off that easily," Antonio replied, with a brilliant smile, as he returned his glass to the bar and then made his way off into the theater.

Colin remained in his place for a moment longer, watching the others file into the main theater. With reluctance, he followed them in and took the steps up to the private box. Soon, he found himself on the inside of the heavy, velvet curtains that enclosed the entrance to the very private space.

"Oh, good, you've made it just in time," his fiancée commented, as she took his hat and placed it on the seat next to her. "The performance is about to start. As you know, it is a new piece titled *Gli Amanti Distanti!*"

"*The Distant Lovers,*" Colin translated. "How charming," he muttered more to himself.

Taking a seat, Colin did everything in his power not to fall asleep during the first part of the performance. What helped him remain alert was his fiancée's inability to remain seated for more than 5 or 10 minutes at a time. By the time she rose for the third round of musical chairs, he decided to stop her to see what was wrong.

"I think it may have been something I ate for breakfast," she muttered.

"Well, we can go," Colin was quick to offer.

"No, please, stay. I would hate for you to miss this," she replied with a sour look on her pale face. "I'll call myself a cab."

"But...," he tried to argue.

"No, if you don't stay and watch the rest for me, I will be very angry with you Colin. I need to know what happens to the hero and his lover," she commanded now, as she fought another wave of nausea.

"Fine, I'll stay. Just go before you turn sick in this box," Colin snapped back.

With a peck on his cheek, she quickly departed.

Sitting, alone, in the secluded box Colin actually started to pay attention to the performance. There, center stage, clad only in a torn loincloth and leather sandals, stood 'the hero.' His bronze, chiseled body was flawless – Colin would give him that – but his flowing mane of thick, black hair was too feminine for his taste. He wondered if it was his actual hair or a wig.

After a few minutes more, he began to listen to the words of the song.

The man was singing of his lover, who had yet to show their face in the performance. As he sang, he made illusions to their beautiful form. He sang of their strength and intelligence, as well as their uncontrollable hold over his own heart and soul. Then he sang of the forbidden nature of their love. That they would have to remain far apart until the time was right for them to live as one.

Colin sat and listened, more intently, translating each word. Oddly enough, he found himself suddenly captivated by the performance. There was something alluring about the actor. Something erotic about the way he touched himself when he spoke about his lover. Something, that actually caused Colin – to his utter surprise – to stir a bit in his tailored pants.

Within seconds of the song's conclusion, the curtains were drawn and the house lights came up. The crowd rose, after a gentle applause, and proceeded to file out into the lobby for a quick intermission.

Colin soon found himself back at the bar, ready to follow up with his drinking partner from earlier in the evening. He needed a hit so that he could calm himself down from what had just occurred in the box. To his knowledge, he had never been as aroused by the sight of another man as he just was.

He stood, anxiously, and waited for several minutes, before nearly giving up. Then, as he was about to head back to his box, he felt a firm hand on his shoulder.

"Going somewhere?" Antonio questioned.

"Uh, oh, no. I was actually just looking for you," Colin replied, as he turned to face the debonair man.

"Ah, ok. How about that quick drink? We still have a few minutes to kill," Antonio responded with a flash of his bright smile.

"Sure," Colin replied, as he led the way back to the bar.

"So, what do you think of the performance so far?" Antonio questioned, as he took his drink from the bar.

"It's ok," Colin commented, as he took a sip of his own drink.

"Just ok, huh?" Antonio replied with a raised eyebrow.

"Yes. Am I missing something?" Colin replied in turn.

"Well, rumor has it that there is a rather shocking ending to this piece," Antonio whispered, as he leaned in closer, so that only Colin could hear him.

"Oh?" Colin replied, edging his way back to put space between the two of them once again.

"Yes. Shocking," Antonio repeated with a wicked smile on his face.

"Well, I guess we will have to wait and see," Colin commented, as he finished his drink.

Just then, the lights pulsed twice signaling the second act.

"Well, it's time," Antonio noted. "We should try to meet up after the performance. I would love to hear what you have to say about the ending."

"Right, so I can tell you if I thought it was truly *shocking* or not," Colin replied.

"Correct. Enjoy the second act," Antonio responded, as he worked his way through the crowd.

Colin made his own way back to his box. Taking his seat, as the lights dimmed, he suddenly heard a slight shuffle to the curtains behind him. Figuring that someone had simply brushed against them, he ignored the noise.

It wasn't until the lights on the stage blazed into action, that he realized he was not alone. Turning, he found himself practically face to face with another man. Startled, he jumped from his seat.

"What the...!" he cried out.

"Pardon me, Sir. I didn't mean to alarm you," the man calmly replied.

"Well, you did. This is a private box. How did you get in here?" Colin snapped back as he eyed the man up and down, attempting to determine if he was a threat or not.

"I simply came through those curtains," the man replied with a gesture of his gloved hand.

"Ah, right, but you don't belong here," Colin retorted in a hushed tone, as he continued to eye the man over, taking in his extremely formal attire of white tie, stiff vest, and tails. He was surprised not to find a cane, cape or top hat at hand.

"I am sorry, Sir. I can go," the man replied with a sorrowful look on his strikingly handsome face.

Colin, sensing a bit of an accent now in the man's voice, stopped him with a firm hand on his forearm.

"No, there is no need for me to be so rude," he suddenly found himself saying. "Please, stay. There is plenty of room for the two of us here," Colin motioned now for the man to take a seat.

"Thank you, Sir. You are very kind," the man replied, as he humbly took a seat, flipping the long tails to his tuxedo jacket behind him as he sat.

"My name is Colin," he noted, as he extended a hand toward the foreign man.

"I am Jean-Luc," the dapper man replied.

"Nice to meet you," Colin responded.

"Shall we enjoy the performance now?" Jean-Luc replied.

"Sure, I suppose we should. Forgive me," Colin noted, as he turned his attention toward the stage.

There, once again, was the muscular, loincloth-clad hero, fighting his way through the evil obstacles of the world, hoping and praying to make the journey safely so that he could be with his lover once again. It was a spectacular presentation, only enhanced by the use of props, set pieces and lighting. Several completely nude actors, wearing nothing but body paints, joined the scenario, posing as the physical manifestations of lies, rumors, mistrust, and ignorance – all evils of the world that were working against the hero, keeping him from his lover.

As the hero continued to clash with these evils, each one proceeded to leave their mark on him. They fought, tumbled, rolled and wrestled, as the hero became more and more covered in colorful streaks representative of each evil.

Colin, sitting on the edge of his seat now, was enraptured. He couldn't take his eyes off of the beautifully shaped figures on the stage. The way they moved, intertwined, and collided with one another – it was mesmerizing. It was titillating.

"You are enjoying this?" Jean-Luc whispered now.

"Yes," Colin found himself replying breathlessly.

"Good, as am I," the man replied, watching Colin more than the actual show.

Colin soon found himself somewhat overheated in his suit. He wondered if he had had one too many to drink. His mind was also quickly growing hazy.

"You look warm," Jean-Luc commented, as he shifted closer to Colin.

"No, I'm...," Colin started, but soon let the words trail away, as he turned to face Jean-Luc.

He suddenly, and shockingly, found himself extremely turned on by the man sitting next to him. Their eyes locked, and Colin couldn't draw himself away. He was enamored, smitten even.

There, before him, was sitting an impeccably suited man. Probably the most beautifully suited man he had ever seen. How could he have ever referred to such an individual as a foul smelling, sardine eating bird? The man was stunning. "Jean-Luc?" Colin called.

"Yes, Colin?" he replied.

"I have...never been," he slowly started, "with another man."

"Well, I would be honored to be your first, Monsieur," the man replied, with a heavier accent than before.

"Would you?" Colin whispered, as he reached out a trembling hand to run it along the man's strong jaw and chin.

"Oui," Jean-Luc whispered back, as he shifted closer, taking the seat that was once occupied by Colin's fiancée. "I promise to be gentle."

"That's what they always say," Colin muttered softly. "Isn't it?"

Jean-Luc moved even closer now, bringing his face mere inches from Colin's own.

"I want to kiss your beautiful lips," Jean-Luc whispered. "May I?"

"Ye-Yes please, I...I would like that," Colin stammered, suddenly feeling a bit awkward in such an intimate setting with such a beautiful man, but he was unwilling to let the moment pass.

With that, Jean-Luc tilted his head, ever so slightly, and leaned in, very slowly, pressing his soft, moistened lips against Colin's own damp, partially parted lips. Colin was tempted to pull away at the last moment, but quickly decided against it. The second he felt Jean-Luc's lips on his own this all-consuming warmth washed over his entire body, starting deep inside his leather shoes and ending at the top of his dark-haired head. Finally, after several minutes of exploring each other's warm mouths, Jean-Luc pulled back, looking Colin directly in the eyes, as he held the man's face in his gloved hands.

"Beau," he whispered.

Colin felt the heat rise along his neck and into his cheeks, flushing them with color.

"You're too kind," he replied, taking in a deep breath, which allowed him to drink in the man's delicious scent.

"And, you are too innocent. This seems wrong," Jean-Luc whispered back.

"No. I'm not and it's not. I promise. Continue," Colin replied, as he put a firm hand on the man's knee.

Jean-Luc, unable to do anything but make love to this charming man before him, did indeed continue.

Running a gloved hand over Colin's jacket, he took the time to savor the cut, fit, and weight of the fabric. Soon, he found himself taking his gloves off to feel the suit. He needed to touch and caress it. He needed to get a good feel for the man within as well.

"Beau," he repeated, as he ran a hand over the lapels of the suit.

"Thank you," Colin sheepishly replied, as he let the man work his hands all over his suited form.

Jean-Luc continued to stroke Colin, running his hands over the exterior of the suit, until one suddenly slipped inside. Moaning ever so slightly, Jean-Luc continued to caress Colin, letting his hand explore the super smooth lining of the jacket. His hand soon found its way to Colin's neat, 5-button vest.

"May I?" Jean-Luc inquired, as he took a single polished button between his fingers.

"Yes," Colin whispered.

Gently, Jean-Luc pushed the top button of the vest through its hole. He continued with two more, until he soon had just enough access to slip inside. As his hand slowly slid within, he found himself trapped between two amazing sensations. One was the slippery smooth sensation that the lining of the vest was producing along the backside of his hand. The other was the buttery smooth sensation that was occurring along the inside of his hand as he let it glide over Colin's pale, silver-grey, silk tie.

"Stupéfier!" Jean-Luc muttered, as he continued to explore Colin's long, perfectly knotted, silk tie.

Running his hand along the length of it, Jean-Luc found himself lost, drawn into its creamy, gorgeous surface. It wasn't until his hand found the impeccable knot at the top that he snapped out of his dream like state.

"Forgive me," Jean-Luc noted, as he pulled back.

"Not at all," Colin replied, as he shifted in his seat a bit, placing a firm hand, once again, on the man's knee.

"I need to kiss you again," Jean-Luc suddenly exclaimed, before leaning in and doing just that.

The two men kissed for longer this time, exploring not only each other's lips, but also now each other's tongues. The two slick masses fought, tangling with one another, until finally one won over the other and made its way further into the opposing man's mouth. This continued for several minutes more, until finally they both felt the need to break away to catch their breath.

"Amazing," Colin muttered breathlessly.

"Indeed," Jean-Luc replied.

The two men took a moment to glance at the stage, for there upon it was the hero of the play lamenting the loss of his lover once again.

As the two watched the stage for a few minutes more, Colin suddenly felt a hand working its way toward the severely tented crotch of his pants. Not wanting to distract Jean-Luc – for the sensation of the man's hand on his crotch was exciting – Colin allowed him the chance to grope and caress his bulge. Soon, Colin felt a tugging and, without glancing down, he understood that that meant his zipper was being slowly slid down. This caused his heart to race a bit and, soon, he found himself taking his eyes from the stage to look upon Jean-Luc once more. He watched as Jean-Luc remained focused on one thing and one thing only – the removal of his thickening manhood from his pants. The Frenchman struggled for the first few seconds, attempting to release the throbbing tool from Colin's boxers, but soon, he had it exposed in all its pulsating glory.

"Merde, Je pense que je Suis dans l'amour...," Jean-Luc muttered now, as he stroked the fat shaft, allowing the pre-cum that was oozing from the cock head to slide out and along the back of his hand.

"My French is good Jean-Luc, but...," Colin attempted to speak, but soon found his words stuck in his throat as the Frenchman skillfully leaned in and took his cock, from tip to base, in one single motion.

"Oh fuck!" Colin muttered, as his throbbing manhood was skillfully devoured in its entirety.

He could feel the man's expert mouth working around the bulbous head of his growing dick. He could sense the wild flicking of his tongue, in and out of his piss slit, working its way along his veined shaft thereafter. He could feel his powerful lips milking the now slick rod, drawing the crystal-clear pre-cum out. He could hear the man slightly moaning as he consumed Colin's cock and juices.

As Jean-Luc continued to work on the oozing tool, Colin fought the urge to bellow even more. He had no desire to draw attention to himself. It was insane – at least to Colin – that this was happening in the first place, but to draw the looks of others would be mortifying. His mind was whirling now with a thousand thoughts, but at the forefront was the question – Why? Was this the culmination of being turned on by the erotic opera below, partnered with the liquor, as well as the subtle advances of the handsome man in the lobby? He desperately tried to reason it out, as he clung to his seat with one hand, bit his tongue and allowed Jean-Luc to continue.

The Frenchman proceeded with this act for several minutes more, relishing in the thickening, drooling tool, until finally, he pulled off and made his way, once again, for Colin's mouth. The two men kissed, ever so passionately, battling with their tongues. "I want you inside me," Jean-Luc finally whispered, as they separated.

"But...," Colin stammered, unable to wrap his intoxicated mind around such an act.

"Yes. I need to feel you deep inside me," Jean-Luc insisted now.

"But, I...," Colin continued to mutter.

"I insist, here and now, you shall make love to me as only a man can," Jean-Luc commanded, as he stood now, drawing Colin out of his chair as well.

The two stood facing one another, with the opera as their backdrop. Colin looked up at Jean-Luc – who was several inches taller – and saw nothing but lust and passion in his dark eyes.

"Do not worry. I shall guide you," Jean-Luc reassured Colin, as he took his hand and squeezed it.

"It's just that…as I've said, I have never been with a man before. Sure I've thought about it, we all do that from time to time, don't we, but I…," Colin's words trailed off now, as Jean-Luc leaned in and kissed him deeply, holding his head in place with one of his massive hands.

Colin soon felt Jean-Luc stroking his exposed cock as they kissed, but, to Colin's surprise, it was not with his bare hand. Instead, the Frenchman was using the silk pocket square – that once resided in Colin's breast pocket – to stroke him. The feel of the smooth fabric, on his slick shaft, was stimulating. It felt cool to the touch and helped to heighten Colin's excitement.

"Please, Monsieur, I need to feel you on the inside. I beg of you. Take me now," Jean-Luc prompted Colin once again.

Colin quickly found his hands on the clasp to Jean-Luc's neatly tailored tuxedo pants.

"No. Slow. I want you, but there is no need to rush this," the Frenchman whispered.

Pausing, Colin removed his hand from the clasp and, instead, proceeded to grope the man through his pants. The thick piece of manhood which was found there, straining against the fabric, held Colin's rapt attention.

"Gentle. There is no need to rub it so hard," Jean-Luc instructed the novice.

Softening his touch, Colin's mind fought, once more, to reason this situation out.

"I know. You are torn. Your emotions are raging. Just take a deep breath and proceed when you feel you can, Mon chéri," Jean-Luc continued to instruct Colin.

Colin, mentally agreeing that he needed more time, paused, and looked up at the dashing, beautifully suited man.

"I'm just not sure…," he muttered now.

"I know, and I am pressuring you. I am sorry," Jean-Luc replied.

"It's not that," Colin whispered. "It's just that, I find myself unable to understand why you would want to be with me. I'm a mere boy in this matter."

"No. You have what I would call – le Coeur d'un explorateur," Jean-Luc replied with a touch of his native tongue.

"I do?" Colin whispered.

"You do. I can see it in your eyes. You have the desire to seek more. To search," Jean-Luc replied, as he moved closer to Colin.

"I...I do," Colin quickly agreed now.

"Then, let us not waste a moment more. I am here for you to discover," Jean-Luc offered, as he took Colin's hands and placed them on the clasp to his pants once more.

Colin, excited now, fumbled at first, but soon found it in himself to undo the man's trousers. Working on the double clasp at the waistband first, he then moved on to the zipper, which was pulled extremely taunt against the manhood found within. Tenderly tugging, Colin did everything in his power not to snap the devise, but soon realized, as he attempted to draw it down, that that was impossible. The zipper gave and, instead of gently opening from the top, split open at the center, causing the zipper tag itself to remain stuck in its position at the top of the teeth, while the rest parted all the way to the other end.

"Intéresser," Jean-Luc muttered, as he watched Colin stare in shock at the sudden predicament.

"I'm sorry," was all that he could muster.

"No need," the Frenchman replied, as he placed his fingers inside the opening and, somewhat violently, ripped it open, snapping the zipper in the process.

"Fuck," Colin exclaimed, due more to the sheer power displayed, than the actual act.

"Continue," Jean-Luc prompted, as he let his pants slowly slide down his legs and pool at his feet.

Colin stood back now and took in the site of Jean-Luc's exposed thighs and calves. He also took the time to stare at his bulging undergarment, which was begging to be removed.

"Libérez la bête!" Jean-Luc whispered.

"Yes," Colin replied, as he licked his lips and reached out for the waistband to the man's silk boxers.

Slowly, without causing another incident, Colin worked the boxers down from around Jean-Luc's narrow waist. There was a moment of panic as the garment was caught up on the massive package held within, but after one or two tugs, the silk rolled over it and the shorts were soon sliding down his legs as well.

Colin couldn't help but gasp as he witnessed the man's cock flop out from behind the fabric. It was beautiful, just as he had expected it would be. The gentle upward curve to the thick, veined shaft was perfect. The plump, hairless balls, which hung below, were also a thing of beauty.

"Take me," Jean-Luc prompted.

Suddenly, overcome with lust, Colin did just that.

Undoing the clasp to his own pants, Colin let them fall to his ankles. In one quick motion, he soon found himself turning Jean-Luc around, lifting the tails to his tuxedo jacket and groping the man's firm, smooth buttocks. He proceeded to slap him in the ass with his dripping cock, while reaching into his jacket pocket to retrieve his leather wallet, which always held a protective rubber. Ripping the packet open, Colin quickly slid it onto his thick, throbbing cock. Grasping the Frenchman's hips, Colin slowly worked his cock toward the dark, hairless hole found deep between the man's masculine and smooth ass cheeks. Jean-Luc, knowing all too well what was coming next, braced himself by grabbing the high back of one of the box seats.

"Doux," he prompted Colin.

As instructed, Colin gently worked his cock into Jean-Luc's eager hole.

It proved difficult at first, since Colin was more accustom to a much larger hole, but soon enough he was slowly sliding into the slightly moist opening. Inch by inch he worked his tool in, until he was up to the thick base. Soon his neatly clipped pubes were brushing against Jean-Luc's bare ass. Sliding out a bit, he quickly worked his way back in, and went deeper still. This elicited a moan from the Frenchman.

Colin continued to work on Jean-Luc's ass, plunging in and out. As he did so, he soon found himself grasping the two tail ends of his very formal tuxedo coat, using them as a rider does riding a horse with a harness. Thrusting in and out, Colin began to moan as well, as Jean-Luc proceeded to flex his tight ass muscles around the throbbing shaft.

"Oui," Jean-Luc grunted, as he clutched the seat before him harder, causing his knuckles to go white.

"Take it," Colin moaned, as he began to thrust even harder now.

"Oui Monsieur," the Frenchman groaned.

It was in this moment that Colin suddenly heard the sound of fabric ripping.

Looking down, he quickly became aware of just how hard he was tugging the tails of Jean-Luc's tuxedo jacket. There, along the center seam, just above the natural vent of the tails, was a split in the coat about 6 inches long that was slowly growing inch by inch with each thrust.

"Merde!" Colin exclaimed, as he continued to power fuck Jean-Luc's tight hole, regardless of the damage he was causing to the man's once flawless formal wear.

"Oui," Jean-Luc moaned, as he rotated his hips in time with the relentless thrusts.

Colin continued to thrust, drilling deeper and deeper.

The feel of the man's hole wrapped around his throbbing cock was astounding! Never in his life had he felt something like this. His mind suddenly raced with even more erotic thoughts of what he wanted to do to this man. Leaning back, Jean-Luc danced upon Colin's cock, rotating his ass so that his cock head could reach previously uncharted areas.

"Take me," Jean-Luc begged. "I'm yours."

Letting go of the jacket tails, Colin reached around the man and started to play with his massive pecs that were encased in the extremely starched, blazing white tuxedo shirt. His fingers hurriedly tugged at the once perfectly hand-tied, white bow at Jean-Luc's throat, undoing it so that he could gain access to the top most button of his shirt. Soon, Colin found his hands on the pearl studs that ran down the front of the crisp bib, and one by one he began popping them open, eager to explore the man's body in full as he fucked him from behind. He fumbled a bit when he hit the stark white vest that was worn over the shirt, but soon he worked the polished buttons on that too and laid it open. Before long, he had both the vest and shirt hanging open, which only left the skin-tight undershirt found within. Unable to control his desire any longer, Colin reached up to the ribbed neckline of the undershirt and proceeded to shred it open, from top to bottom, exposing Jean-Luc's flawlessly smooth pecs – which he massaged and groped now, as he continued to thrust into the man's ass.

"Take my hole and make it your own. Mark me as yours," Jean-Luc breathlessly instructed Colin.

Thrusting wildly, Colin did just that. Within seconds, he was exploding inside the rubber, inside the Frenchman's ass. Hot, thick, and ridiculously abundant, Colin's creamy load quickly filled the rubber to its limit. Jean-Luc could feel the mass building in his ass. A smile slid across his parched lips as he felt this.

Pushing him forward now, to lean upon the back of the chair, Colin rested along Jean-Luc's broad back. He took a moment to catch his breath, as he slowed and ceased his wild thrusts. Withdrawing his cock was difficult, at first, and not because of any physical complications, it was more a mental barrier that was causing him a problem. Colin wished he could remain inside of Jean-Luc forever. The feeling of his throbbing cock inside of such an individual was overwhelming. It was intimate beyond words. It was everything he dreamed it would be and so much more.

"Jean-Luc?" Colin muttered into the man's ear, that was mere inches from his mouth now.

"Oui?" he replied, still gasping for his breath.

"I think...," Colin whispered.

"Oui?" he questioned once more.

"Je pense que je Suis tombé pour toi," Colin replied in his best French.

"Oui Monsieur, you have fallen. But, as we both know, that can not be," Jean-Luc noted with a sorrowful tone in his voice.

"Why?" Colin abruptly replied, as he softened and slowly slid out of the man now.

"Because, we are merely two ships passing in the night," Jean-Luc replied.

"That's shit and you know it!" Colin found himself barking in return, as he ripped off the seed filled rubber, splashing its contents all over Jean-Luc's dress pants and shoes, as he tossed it to the floor of the booth.

"Shh, Monsieur. Someone will hear you," Jean-Luc replied, as he put a hand to Colin's mouth.

"No," Colin bellowed now as he turned away, suddenly caught up in a flood of emotions.

"We shall meet again, Monsieur, worry not. But, you know nothing more can happen now," Jean-Luc whispered into Colin's ear.

"I...," Colin stammered, as his eyes were suddenly drawn to the stage below.

There, in the center of the stage was the hero of the opera, cradling the seemingly lifeless form of his lover, which he sang to now. Colin's eyes went to the form resting in the hero's massive arms. It was the form of a nude, young man, stunning in every way – so absolutely stunning that the image took Colin by surprise.

"Jean-Luc. Look...," Colin stated, as he twisted to look upon the gorgeous Frenchman, but, when he turned, the man was gone.

"Jean-Luc?" Colin muttered, as he quickly and foolishly looked around the small space of the box.

Returning his gaze to the stage once more the emotions that were flooding in now overtook him and he soon found himself uncontrollably weeping.

He wept for the hero of the opera who fought and struggled to return to his lover.

He wept for the dead lover, who was even more remote now – hence, the title, *The Distant Lovers*.

He wept because Jean-Luc was gone and he was all alone.

Then, oddly, his tear-filled eyes were drawn to something in the box. Stepping toward the item, which was glinting now in the light of the stage, Colin took a hold of it and brought it about to get a better look. There, in his hand, was a skillfully crafted walking stick. Engraved in the silver knob, at the top of the long, black cane, were the initials JLB.

"Jean-Luc," Colin muttered, with a twinge of hope in his heart.

It was at this moment, that the crowd below proceeded to give the performers of the opera a standing ovation.

Colin's heart soared at the sound.

"We will meet again," Colin whispered. "Mon beau fantôme."

Bait & Switch

As Antonio stepped out from the warm interior of the Metropolitan Opera House he removed his black, lambskin leather gloves from the deep, silk-lined pockets of his thick, cashmere coat. He then proceeded to work them onto his masculine, yet beautifully manicured hands, adjusting one or two of his rings along the way.

"Ah. What a night!" he exclaimed, to no one in particular.

Strutting down the main steps of the performance house, Antonio could not help but feel stimulated and alive. The performance he had just witnessed had been both mesmerizing and erotic. Actually, the entire evening was turning out to be sheer perfection and it filled him with great pleasure. Antonio was looking hot in his brand new, perfectly tailored tuxedo, he had a wallet filled with cash just aching to be blown and he was feeling particularly playful.

Pausing for a moment on the edge of the main courtyard near one of the many fountains Antonio scanned the crowd of departing patrons. He hoped, but doubted, that he would spot someone he knew. Perhaps, he thought, the young, suited stud he had shared a drink with earlier in the evening would meet up with him, even if it meant that his fiancée had to join them. The night was young; he was edging for a good time and was hoping to do it in the company of another.

It was not until he was just about to give up his search that a deep and seductive voice from behind him played across his ears.

"So, sexy, where are you heading tonight?" the male voice asked.

Before Antonio turned he immediately knew from the smooth

tone who had spoken these words.

"Ricardo, my friend," Antonio responded, as he turned to face the man now.

"Antonio, you stud," Ricardo replied, taking his friend into his arms to apply a very firm and intense hug.

"How are you?" Antonio questioned, as he pulled back now to get a good look at his friend.

"I'm doing well. Very well," Ricardo noted, as he too pulled back to eye his friend up and down.

"Damn, look at you. You are one hot mother fucker," Antonio barked, as he took inventory of the man standing before him.

"Yeah, well, you are not so bad yourself," Ricardo barked back with a wicked smirk on his thick lips.

The two men stood now and allowed their eyes to work upon one another.

Antonio was never disappointed when he looked upon the image of his friend Ricardo – tall, dark and irresistibly handsome, the man was drool-worthy. With a beautiful head of thick, jet-black hair that brushed his broad shoulders, piercing blue eyes that spoke to the soul and smooth, lick-able, sun kissed skin, the man was a vision to behold and lust over. Antonio, having spent countless hours in the gym with him, also knew that every inch of Ricardo's 6'3" frame was sculpted to near perfection under his precisely tailored garments.

As Ricardo stood before him, Antonio – almost unable to believe it possible – was startled even more by his captivating good looks. The man was dressed to the nines from head to toe. Antonio could only assume, dressed as he was, that his friend was coming from the same formal venue.

"Enjoy the show?" Antonio questioned, as he continued to give his friend the once over.

"Perhaps," Ricardo replied, as he remained in his place, allowing his friend the pleasure of ogling him in public.

"Good, but you should have told me you were coming. We could have come together," Antonio commented, as he continued along his visual feast.

What struck Antonio most about Ricardo's appearance was the beautiful, thick, black leather trench coat that he wore over his tuxedo.

It framed the tailored suit to perfection. The scent of the leather was intoxicating too and it mixed delightfully with Ricardo's heady cologne. The combination was perfect for a man so strikingly masculine and butch. With his top coat, Ricardo wore a long, white, silk scarf, as well as a pair of black leather gloves – two perfect additions that only enhanced the overall look more.

"I'm sorry. It was a last minute decision," Ricardo replied, as he belted up his leather trench. "Shall we continue this discussion over drinks?"

"Sure, why not?" Antonio responded, as he belted his own thick top coat.

As the two men strode down the last set of steps leading to the main sidewalk their attention turned to a disturbance at the curb. There, before them was a construction crew packing things up for the night. It appeared to Antonio that the crew had been working on one of the many recently formed sinkholes, which were a product of the heavy rains they had had over the last week. The city currently seemed to need an around-the-clock crew when it came to maintenance and repairs.

"Damn, I'd hate to be working this late at night," Ricardo commented.

"I know. It's a shame, isn't it?" Antonio replied, as he proceeded to skirt the area where the men were loading their equipment into a utility truck.

Ricardo made a move to follow his friend when, suddenly, one of the construction workers started in on him.

"Hey, mother fucker, watch where you are going!" the filthy, blue-collar grunt barked.

"Uh, excuse me asshole, but there's no need to mouth off at me. I can see you and your pack," Ricardo replied, as he took a step back and away.

"Well fucker, I can smell you coming a mile away. Ya may want to cut back on the cologne dude," the guy replied, as he stepped closer to Ricardo.

"Yeah, well, you may want to invest in some. You smell like the sewer you crawled out of," Ricardo barked back.

"Hey! Knock it off guys. Cool it Dick. Leave the guy alone," a second construction worker suddenly shouted.

"Damn, Vin, I was just playing with the guy," Dick barked back to Vinny, his co-worker, as he kept his fierce gaze on Ricardo.

"Yeah, Ricardo, let's go," Antonio suddenly stepped in and pulled his friend away.

"Yeah, Ricardo, go off and play with your pretty boyfriend," Dick muttered just loud enough for Antonio to hear.

"Don't let that jerk get to you man," Antonio commented, as he escorted Ricardo across the street. "He's just envious," he continued, feeling the intense stare of Dick on their backs.

"Yeah, you're right, I can't let it get to me, but some guys...," Ricardo replied, clenching his gloved hands into fists.

"I know man. I know. Say no more. Just fuck it. Let's focus on getting our private party for two started. I've got a wallet full of cash just burning a hole in my pocket," Antonio noted.

"Nice," Ricardo replied, as a grin returned to his full lips.

As the two men strode down the sidewalk, keeping pace with one another both men couldn't help but notice the glances they were getting from those passing by.

"Jeez, you'd think these people have never seen two sharp dressed men walking together," Ricardo noted.

"Uh, I have a feeling it's not the two of us they are checking out, but him...," Antonio replied, as he raised a gloved hand and pointed to the street.

There, sitting in the open flatbed of the utility truck – which was now slowly moving down the street – was the obnoxious construction worker, Dick, making obscene gestures and faces at Ricardo and Antonio.

"Fuck, this guy just doesn't give up," Ricardo barked as he glared at the guy who had undone the zipper to his work coverall and was now flashing his very fleshy testicles at the two of them while licking his lips and making vulgar sucking sounds.

"Come on, this guy is absolutely nuts. Let's get off of the street and inside. We can wash away that alarming image with a drink or two," Antonio replied, as he sized up the street and scanned it for the nearest drinking establishment.

"Sure, that sounds good to me. I guess any place will do for now,"

Ricardo commented, as he led Antonio through the closest door, keeping one eye on the utility truck as it rolled to a stop just down the street.

Within minutes of entering the bar, the two formally dressed men could tell that their situation, and probably their entire evening, was rapidly deteriorating.

"Uh, maybe we should look for another place to have a drink," Antonio commented to Ricardo as they foolishly went deeper into the dim, smoke-filled room.

They could feel many sets of eyes watching them as they awkwardly approached the edge of the bar. Oddly enough the two handsome men – normally the center of attention and comfortable in almost any situation – suddenly felt very out of place, but Ricardo wasn't willing to give in so easily.

"No," Ricardo replied as he unbelted his leather trench. "I need a drink pretty badly now. This place will have to do, not to mention the fact that that freak is still out there. I saw his truck slow down as we entered this place."

"Damn. You're kidding me." Antonio replied with a look of concern on his face.

"No man, I wish I was," Ricardo stated, as he turned now to place his order with the surly bartender who was quickly growing impatient with them.

"Can I get a vodka scotch?" Ricardo asked the gruff bartender.

"I don't know. Can you?" the bartender replied with a snicker as he eyed the two formally dressed studs up and down.

"Well, I guess that's up to you," Antonio interjected, as he slid his leather gloves off.

"Yeah, I guess it is," the bartender snorted, "that and a lot more," he added with a depraved grin.

"Uh, can I just get my drink?" Ricardo questioned with an edge of attitude in his deep voice.

"Yeah, I'll get right on that Mr. Bond. Shaken, not stirred. I got it," the bartender replied with a sneer, as he turned away.

"Damn, this is not the night I was hoping for," Antonio commented, as he looked around the seedy bar, taking note of the rough and tough atmosphere.

"Well, we can hit the road right after I bang back this drink and hopefully that lunatic will be gone when we get outside," Ricardo commented, as his dark eyes locked with Antonio's.

"A lunatic, huh?" a booming voice from behind them suddenly barked.

As the two formal studs slowly turned to view the origin of this outburst they suddenly found themselves face to face with Dick, as well as his co-worker Vinny.

The two blue-collar grunts stood only inches apart and just a few feet away from Antonio and Ricardo. They were no longer wearing their work coveralls; instead, they were both dressed in their sweaty street clothes.

Dick was in a pair of tight and torn, black-colored jeans, as well as a white, cotton wife beater that he wore like a second skin on his ample upper-body muscles. On his feet he had on a pair of black leather boots. Slung over his shoulder was a black, leather biker jacket.

Vinny was also in a pair of jeans, but his were a faded blue and they encased his well-muscled legs to perfection. Upon his upper body, he wore a cotton tank top that was stretched to its very limit across rock hard muscles. He also had on a pair of traditional, tan-colored work boots, as well as a brown, leather jacket grasped in one of his oversized work-worn paws.

The two men, if cleaned up, were probably very handsome – gorgeous even – but at the end of an intense workday that was difficult to tell upon first glance. With their skin coated in a layer of grit and their hair slicked back, soaked in sweat, they were far from attractive, although, truth be told, there was a certain animalistic appeal to their current look.

Dick's hair was thick, dark and wavy, framing his face like a mane, with the damp, stringy tips brushing upon his broad shoulders as he shifted his gaze. He had a five-o-clock shadow running along his firm jaw-line, which only helped to draw attention to his sensual, full lips. His eyes, framed in dark, long lashes were the color of the night sky. His skin, while callused in spots from hard labor, was a beautiful tan color from hours in the sun. In his left ear he wore two gold hoops.

Vinny was the fairer of the two, with spiked, golden-blond hair and pale, sky-blue eyes. He too wore a five-o-clock shadow, but his was far more subtle in its appearance, allowing his thick, rosebud lips to stand out on their own. He had a cleft in his strong chin and dimples that appeared out of nowhere when he smirked, which was what he was doing now.

"My buddy asked you a question," Vinny commented now as he leaned in to get a better look at the two visibly shaken men. "I think you better answer him because this time, unlike out on the street, I'm not playing the peacekeeper. This time I'm gonna let him rip into you, while I sit back and watch."

"Uh, listen guys, we don't want any trouble," Antonio blurted out as he moved between Dick and Ricardo, keeping an eye on Vinny.

"Well, pretty boy, then your buddy better give me a damn good answer as to why he's calling me a lunatic," Dick barked back, as he poked Antonio square in the center of his tuxedo clad chest, leaving a faint smudge on the stark white material of his crisp, freshly starched shirt.

"He was just surprised by your actions out on the street. You have to admit, they were not what we would call normal public behavior," Antonio quickly replied, with an air of caution in his voice.

"Oh, normal you say?" Dick spat back, as he moved even closer, his hot breath washing over Antonio's smooth skin, as one of his free hands subconsciously groped the bulging crotch of his dark jeans.

"What exactly *is* normal?" Vinny questioned, sizing Ricardo and Antonio up.

"Yeah, come on boys. I mean, with the two of you dressed the way you are, standing here in the middle of a leather bar...is that what you would consider normal?" Dick inquired, with a doubtful look on his face.

"Hey, Dick," the bartender suddenly interjected. "You better watch how you talk to these two guys. Do you know who the blond one is?"

"Uh, no, Buck I have no idea. Would you care to shed some light on the situation?" Dick replied, as he crossed his massive arms over his equally massive pecs.

"That there is the Police Chiefs son. Tony I believe it is," Buck replied, as he pointed to Antonio.

"Oh really...," Dick murmured, stroking his crotch a bit further down the leg now.

"Well, that makes this situation even better," Vinny added. "I'm sure your super-butch Dad wouldn't want to hear about how his only son was seen playing around in a leather bar."

"Come on guys, really, let's not start any trouble. All we want is a drink and to be left alone," Antonio replied, with a dead serious look on his handsome face.

"Well, first of all, your friend still hasn't given me a good reason why he's walking around calling me a lunatic and second, I'm not sure the two of you realize the situation you have put yourselves in," Dick commented now with a wicked grin on his thick lips.

"Yeah," Vinny added, "it seems that the two of you are going nowhere. At least not dressed like that you're not. I mean, come on guys, you certainly can't just walk out those doors and act like nothing happened in here. If my hunch is right Buck here has already called his reporter friend and he's on his way over, ready to snap some pics the moment you two get outside."

Antonio locked eyes with the sleazy bartender and from the look on his face he knew this to be true.

"Shit," Antonio muttered, looking to Ricardo now as he anxiously ran a hand through his neatly styled, thick, blond-brown hair.

Ricardo, quietly and quickly sizing up their situation, was unable to put Antonio's mind at ease and, instead, just shrugged inside of his thick, leather trench coat.

"That's right boys. Admit you have lost this round and just give in," Vinny taunted them both. "It will only help to make this evening more enjoyable for all of us."

"Right, I mean, come now, do you honestly expect us to believe that the two of you 'accidentally' stumbled into this dive?" Dick questioned Antonio.

"Believe what you want fuckers! We're leaving," Ricardo suddenly spat as he grabbed Antonio by the arm and proceeded to push him toward the nearest exit.

"I wouldn't do that if I were you," Buck shouted to the two of them as they broke through the front door and out onto the street.

Within seconds of exiting the bar, Antonio and Ricardo found themselves caught in the stark white blasts of a photographers flash.

"Shit," Antonio cursed as he stumbled back into the bar, practically dragging Ricardo with him.

"Fuck, we can't leave. We're fucking trapped man," Ricardo spat, as he leaned against a nearby table.

"So it seems," Dick interjected, as he approached the two startled men. "So, I think the two of you need to make yourselves comfortable. Let's start with taking off these beautiful coats. What do you say?"

With that, Vinny stepped in and proceeded to undo the belt on Antonio's cashmere coat, as Dick did the same to Ricardo's trench, only after sliding the white silk scarf from around his neck.

"Don't fight us. Look around. We outnumber you guys and you know it," Dick muttered into Ricardo's ear, as he slid the thick leather coat from his tuxedoed body. "I'll take those pretty leather gloves too," Dick added with a grin.

The two friends locked eyes at this point, and each man knew – without speaking a single word – they needed to play along or things would get horrifically worse – if that was even possible. Ricardo inwardly decided it was, as he slid the skin-tight gloves from his hands and passed them to the filthy bastard.

"There we go. Isn't that better?" Vinny questioned the two men. "Now, let's talk about how we are going to go about enjoying ourselves this evening."

"Yeah," Dick added, "I think it may be time to play a game. What do you think?"

"Sure," Vinny replied. "What do you have in mind?"

"It's a game I like to call 'Gear Shift'," Dick responded, as he eyed the two formal studs up and down.

"I see. How does that one go Dick?" Vinny replied, as he took a step closer to Antonio, drinking in the man's masculine cologne.

"Well, let's start by inspecting the playing pieces," Dick responded with a smirk on his face. "Let's see if this is going to work."

"Ok," Vinny eagerly replied. "Shoot. What do I need to do?"

"First, we need to get some measurements on our two boys here," Dick spoke, with a much more serious look on his face, inspecting them intently.

"Measurements?" Vinny questioned now, somewhat confused.

"Yeah, we need to figure out which one of these two young studs is better suited – pun intended – for each of us."

"I don't understand Dick," Vinny continued to question. "What sort of game is this? I thought we were going to get it on with these guys."

"Oh, we will. Trust me," Dick replied with a wicked smile on his lips and a somewhat wild look in his eyes.

As Antonio and Ricardo stood, waiting for the two guys to shut the hell up and get started doing whatever it was they were going to do to them, they both noticed that the other men in the room were now watching with great enjoyment and anticipation.

"Uh, do you know what the hell they are talking about?" Ricardo whispered to Antonio.

"No, but I have a hunch we're going to find out soon enough," Antonio replied, suddenly feeling very self-conscious.

"Ok, listen up," Dick suddenly barked to the anxious crowd. "These two tuxed up studs are going to strip down to their birthday suits. Got it? Then Vin and I are going to do the same. After the four of us are bare ass naked, we are going to swap clothes – hence, the title of this game: Gear Shift."

"Fuck yeah," Vinny replied. "I'd love to suit up real sharp and strut around town man."

"Exactly, although, we are going to have some group fun, once we swap gear," Dick continued to explain his plan.

"Nice man. I love the way you think," Vinny replied with a broad grin as he stepped closer to Antonio and ran a rough hand along the smooth fabric of his tuxedo jacket sleeve.

"So, spill those measurements boys. I have a hunch that this is going to work out perfectly," Dick barked, as he approached Ricardo, meeting him eye to eye.

"Damn, quit the gab and get it on already," spat one of the drunken guys as he sat watching this scenario play out.

"Calm down fucker. Don't you understand the art of foreplay? You'll get what's coming to you," Dick barked in return, as he locked eyes with Ricardo once more.

"So, tell me, you're about 6'3", right?" Dick questioned.

Ricardo nodded.

"You weigh about 280...285?" Dick continued.

Ricardo nodded again.

"Nice. Perfect. Same here. I figure you have about a 33 or 34-inch waist, and those pecs have got to be a size 54 or so. Am I right?"

"Yes," Ricardo verbally confirmed now.

"Excellent man," Dick replied with a big shit eating grin.

"What about you?" Vinny questioned Antonio now. "You're roughly 6'2" and weigh about 275. No?"

Antonio nodded.

"Waist 32? Pecs 50?"

"Yeah," Antonio replied.

"Fuck. Just like me," Vinny barked. "Give an inch or two."

"See, boys, was that so hard?" Dick questioned them both. "Now, strip!"

With this command, the room went wild. Leather-clad men of every shape, size and color started hooting and hollering, begging for the show to begin. Antonio and Ricardo stood for several minutes, unable, at first, to respond to the order, worried about where this was quickly headed.

"Didn't you hear me?" Dick barked. "Get those fuckin' suits off or Vinny and I will strip them off of you and it won't be pretty."

Antonio looked to Ricardo to see if he was going to agree to this or if they should attempt to bolt, regardless of who was waiting outside for them. As Ricardo's hand went to the buttons on his double-breasted tuxedo jacket Antonio knew what the answer was.

"There we go," Dick commented as he watched Ricardo slide out of his neatly tailored jacket, exposing a pair of black suspenders with silver clips and a smooth, perfectly pleated, silk cummerbund in black, which flawlessly encased his narrow waist.

Antonio stood and watched as Ricardo walked toward Dick and handed him the jacket.

"It's your turn," Vinny prompted.

Antonio hesitated for yet a minute more. He wasn't sure he could do this, but then he looked around and figured if he didn't do this himself the hungry crowd would do it for him. So, grasping the buttons of his single-breasted tuxedo jacket, one at a time, he undid them and slid it off as well. The next thing he knew he was handing it over to Vinny.

"Excellent," Dick barked as he handled Ricardo's jacket, running a rough hand over the silky smooth, silver-colored lining.

"More!" yelled one of the leather-clad guys.

"Yeah, take it all off!" yet another guy shouted.

Ricardo was the first one to unfasten the clasp to his cummerbund, stripping it off and handing it over to Dick. Then, he worked the taut suspenders off his broad shoulders and let them dangle at his side, leaving them clipped to the satin waistband of his pants. Next, he worked on the silver and black, diamond-encrusted cufflinks, which held his double wide French cuffs in place. Lastly, he tugged at the meticulously tied silk bow, situated at his throat, letting it pop undone and lay across his powerful chest.

Dick reached up at this point with a calloused hand and slowly undid the top button of Ricardo's lay-down collared shirt. He then proceeded to work on each stud until Ricardo's shirt was splayed open all the way down to his tapered waist. Once he had this completed he proceeded to run his rough hand inside the opening, groping Ricardo's meaty pecs through his tight cotton undershirt.

"Who's the lunatic now?" Dick muttered to Ricardo, as he felt the two nipple rings, just below the smooth, slightly damp fabric of his shirt.

"A stuck up bitch like you, pierced? I find that hard to believe," Dick commented as he continued to run his hand over the bumps, until finally rolling the undershirt up to expose not only the most stunning set of washboard abs, but also the meatiest, pierced pecs he'd ever seen.

"Damn, boys, I think we have ourselves a kinky one here," Dick bellowed, as he stood back to let the others see the rings.

With more hoots and hollers from the crowd Dick proceeded to strip Ricardo of his undone bow tie, crisp tuxedo shirt and tight undershirt, which left him, at this point, standing only in his perfectly tailored pants, silk socks and highly polished, leather shoes.

"Ok, back to you," Vinny noted, as he poked Antonio in the chest.

Once again Antonio took pause to assess the situation. His mind whirled with the thoughts of this filthy grunt suiting up in his very expensive and meticulously cared for gear. He wasn't sure he could witness such an act.

"I said...your turn buddy," Vinny prodded him again.

"Ok, calm down," Antonio barked back, as he proceeded to undo his silk cummerbund, followed by his black suspenders with their golden clips.

After handing both items over to Vinny, Antonio proceeded to undo his gold and diamond cufflinks, slipping each one from its place in his stiff French cuffs.

"Nice. Continue...," Vinny commented as he watched with an admiring eye.

Antonio continued to undress, removing his hand-tied, silk bow tie, with one flick of his wrist. He then proceeded to undo the matching gold studs, in place, down the front of his beautifully pressed, arrow-collared shirt. One by one Antonio popped out the studs and, in turn, handed them over to Vinny.

"Keep going stud," Vinny taunted him. "Off with the shirt."

At this point Antonio figured he had nothing to loose. He knew he had an amazing, perfectly sculpted body under all of this gear so why not give the guys a show, he suddenly thought to himself!

After stripping the tuxedo shirt off he proceeded to grab the neck of his undershirt and in one hard tug he ripped it down the center, shredding it in the process and exposing his hard, muscular upper body.

"Fuck," Vinny muttered, "You may have the kinky one, but I think I got the wilder one of the two."

"Nice," Dick commented, watching the show along with the rest of the bar.

Antonio stood now, breathing heavily, with his slightly damp muscles rippling and flexing for all to see.

"Ok, now for the pants. Both of you at the same time," Dick barked, taking a long swig of a beer Buck provided him with.

Antonio and Ricardo looked to one another and for some reason the two of them started to get into this scenario, acknowledging this turn of events with a mutual grin. There was suddenly something very erotic and appealing about stripping for a room full of animalistic leather fuckers.

Ricardo made the first move and popped the clips of his suspenders. After getting them free he swung them in the air and directed them toward Dick, releasing them mid-swing. They struck Dick square in the chest, to which, he let out an approving growl with a wicked smile on his face.

Antonio, having already removed his suspenders started to undo his neatly tailored pants, one clasp at a time, until it was the moment to draw the zipper down. Ricardo, seeing that Antonio was on the verge of shedding his pants followed suit and undid the clasps on his pants tugging on his zipper as well.

At the same time the two men slid their zippers down and, within seconds, they both had their neatly pressed pants pooling around their ankles. The room thundered with grunts and growls, as most guys leaned in to get a better look at their newfound 'entertainers.'

Ricardo had on a pair of tight, black bikini briefs, which only helped to draw attention to his muscular thighs, as well as blatantly present his full package. Antonio was much more subtle in his choice of underwear, sporting a pair of white, silk boxers which hugged the firm globes of his very muscular and very full ass beautifully.

"Nice. Fuckin' nice." Dick barked as he licked his lips and groped his crotch.

Antonio and Ricardo both took a moment to step out of their pants, each bending to pick them up and then hand them to their respective playing 'partners.' As they stood now, wearing nothing but their underwear, sheer socks and leather dress shoes the crowd proceeded to ogle, bark, whistle and howl at the two very exposed men.

"How about if we get them to serve us some drinks?" one of the drunk, leather-clad studs called out.

"Yeah," Buck barked in agreement. "That would be hot." "No," Dick replied. "This isn't about humiliating these studs; it's about bringing them down a peg or two to our level. I wanna give them a taste of a rougher life, not completely degrade them."

"Ya saying my job is humiliating?" Buck shot back, as, ironically, he proceeded to hand one of the drunks a trashcan to vomit in.

"Well come on, it isn't exactly the life of luxury," Vinny interjected with a dry smile on his face and a glance toward the vomiting patron.

"I suppose that's true," Buck replied, with a smirk on his lips.

"Ok, enough gabbing," Dick suddenly barked. "Continue!"

Antonio looked to Ricardo now, wondering if he was going to go the full mile and strip off his briefs. Within seconds he had his answer.

Ricardo placed one finger from each hand into the waistband of his bikini briefs and in one quick – almost professional move – he had them off and swinging in his hand. The crowd roared at the site of this muscular demigod with his amazingly long cock swinging between his rock hard legs. As he walked toward Dick, presenting his briefs to the guy, his still flaccid cock swung back and forth, causing his smooth, oversized balls to bounce as well.

"Fuckin' a, you're beautiful," Dick moaned as he took the briefs into his paw and then brought them up to his nose to drink in the scent left there.

Antonio watched this display and hoped he could follow through with his end of the game. Hesitating for the final time he proceeded to work his boxers off, sliding them down his muscular legs until they were finally around his ankles. Once again the crowd of men howled and whistled, crying out for more. All eyes were on him now, as no one was able to look away from his massive, semi-erect cock, which was oozing a thick stream of crystal-clear pre-cum.

"Shit," Vinny moaned.

At this point even Ricardo had to take in the image of his friend. Antonio's smooth, muscular, masculine body was incredibly beautiful, down to the very last inch of his throbbing, drooling cock.

"Bravo," Buck exclaimed from behind the bar.

Vinny stepped closer to Antonio now and hesitated for a brief moment before bending over to help him step out of his boxers. Following Dick's lead Vinny brought the slightly moist shorts to his mouth and proceeded to lick the drops of pre-cum that were found all over the inside of the crotch.

"Hmm, tasty," Vinny moaned.

"Ok, last two items on the menu, your shoes and socks," Dick demanded.

With that, Ricardo took his place next to Antonio and the two men proceeded to slide their shoes off and then, very slowly, their sheer, over the calf socks. Once the two men were completely naked they proceeded to hand over these last few items. At this point Dick and Vinny took a moment to drink in the sight of their two, very muscular, and surprisingly masculine 'playing pieces.'

"Nice. Who would have guessed the two of you were so damn

butch and playful even," Dick grunted, then continued, "I usually tend to ignore men in suits, but from now on, I'm gonna have to keep an eye on guys like you."

"Yeah," Vinny added, as his eyes washed over the two exposed studs, "who would have guessed?"

"Ok, enough about them. Now it's our turn to show these guys what we are made of," Dick commented before he finished his beer.

The crowd cheered and barked their fellow leather studs into action.

"Come on Dick! Take it off!" one guy hollered.

"Yeah, Vinny, take it all off baby!" another grunted.

With that the two men took center stage, pushing Antonio and Ricardo to the side. Then, slowly and somewhat erotically, they removed their worn, soiled, street clothes.

Dick was rather quick in getting himself down to his skivvies. His wife beater was off in a flash, exposing his massive, slightly hairy pecs. Next, he kicked his leather boots off, one at a time, only to reveal the soaking wet socks held within. He paused for only a moment, allowing Vinny to catch up with him, but by the time he was ready to drop his, Dick was almost finished with sliding his tight, slightly torn jeans down to around his ankles.

"Yeah!" Buck barked.

Vinny glanced over as he finished removing his own work-worn jeans and couldn't help but pause and take notice of his amazingly butch co-worker.

On hot summer days he'd seen Dick shirtless and always admired his chiseled abs and massive pecs, but now that he was standing in only a leather jockstrap, Vinny soon began to realize that there was much more to admire in the man.

There, resting neatly between his thick, hardened thighs was the largest bulge Vinny had ever seen. He was amazed that Dick could keep it so well hidden inside of his very tight jeans, because now that is was almost out in the open, the monster held within seemed enormous.

"Fuck man, you sure know how to live up to a name," Vinny barked, as he continued to eye up Dick's package.

"Yep. They didn't deem me Dick for nothing. I'm all dick. All of the time," he replied with a big shit eating grin on his face.

As Vinny stood now, mere inches away from the yet to be seen slab of meat inside of Dick's jock, he was tempted to tell the other two guys to fuck off so that he and Dick could have some fun of their own.

"I know what you're thinking man," Dick suddenly turned and spoke to Vinny directly, "but it's not going to happen. We have two perfectly able studs waiting for us to play with and, damn it, we are going to get it on with them. We'll have time to play one-on-one later. Now, let's strip these shorts and socks off and start suiting up in their gear!"

"Yeah," Buck exclaimed from the bar, as he sorted through the formal gear, laying it out for Dick and Vinny, "get on with it already!"

With that, Dick and Vinny rolled off their sweat soaked socks and tossed them at Ricardo and Antonio.

"Take a good long sniff on those wet boys," Dick barked.

"Ok," Vinny noted now, as he worked his fingers into the waistband of his boxer briefs, "you ready?"

"Shit yeah man. Just wait until you see the reaction of the crowd," Dick replied.

"Let me go first man," Vinny begged, knowing that he couldn't compete with the monster inside of Dick's leather pouch.

"Sure, buddy, go for it," Dick replied, as he took a step back.

Standing on his own now, Vinny slowly worked his damp, slightly worn cotton boxers down off his narrow hips and then across his ample thighs. The moment he did that his fully erect, beautifully cut cock popped up and slapped his rock hard abs. The generous curve of his thick penis was somewhat shocking. It nearly formed a perfect 'O' as it sprang up from its massive base, bending back further and further, until the tip of his now dripping cock lay against his pierced belly button.

"Damn, size may be one thing, but you get points for style man," Dick barked.

"Thanks man. Now it's your turn," Vinny replied, as he stroked his cock a bit.

Dick took center stage now, looking around the room, egging the other guys on.

"Come on men. What do ya say? Wanna see some Dick tonight?" he yelled.

The howls, barks and whistles were enough of a reply to get him going.

Turning, with his bare ass to Ricardo and Antonio – who were now leaning against the bar watching this spectacle – Dick proceeded to tauntingly play with the elastic straps to his jock. As he drew the very tight, wide band away from his hips he had to tug the leather pouch over his massive, ever growing bulge, until finally he let his thick slab of cock meat flop out and over the waistband. Several guys situated in the front of the crowd gasped. Others, standing in the rear fought to get a better view, but soon realized that they too could make out every massive inch of his throbbing, gorgeous cock.

"Shit," Buck moaned, "now that's a cock to be reckoned with!"

"Does it have a name?" one drunken guy questioned.

"Shit, it probably has its own mailing address," another barked.

Dick stood there now, completely naked, and watched as the men ogled and drooled and fawned all over him.

"Ok boys, now for the real fun. Time to suit up!" Dick shouted as he strode toward the bar where Buck had neatly set out the two previously formal studs gear.

"Nice job," he commented to the bartender, who seemed eager to assist in the process of dressing, "but I think the boys here need to give Vin and I a little instruction as to how a proper man suits up."

With that, Antonio and Ricardo stepped closer and joined Vinny and Dick at the side of the bar. At this point they both realized there was no need to escape this situation. Without a word spoken the two men had decided that this could actually be enjoyable on many different levels.

"Well, first of all, you would shower and shave, but I'm not sure that that is going to happen here this evening," Antonio noted as he ran a hand over the items lying on the bar.

"True," Dick replied. "That's not going to happen. So, what's next?"

"Well, I believe each man is rather particular in his dressing habits, but I will go with what works best for me," Antonio replied. "I believe we will be suiting you up in Ricardo's gear?" he questioned now.

"Yeah, the two of us seem better suited, as in body shape and size," Dick noted with a very serious look on his face.

"Correct," Antonio now noted, as he reached for Ricardo's skimpy bikini briefs, "although, somehow I don't think these will work on you."

"Hmm, let's see," Dick replied as he took the briefs into his paws and attempted to try them on. Within seconds, both men knew that they were excessively small, as they barely did justice to covering his colossal, extremely hairy balls, let alone the monster that swung above them.

"They are a little snug, but they're holding the twins rather nicely," Dick replied as he adjusted the thin waistband straps, allowing his thick cock to dangle freely.

"Hmm, well, that's not really the look we are going for here, but, if you want to keep them on that's fine," Antonio commented.

At this point Ricardo couldn't help but look down at his flaccid cock and worry that he just wasn't measuring up to the others regardless of the fact that his cock measured well over 9 inches.

"Ok, now for your socks. They can and, I feel, should be sheer and able to roll up and over your calves. These are known as OTCs," Antonio instructed Dick as he picked up Ricardo's discarded socks.

Antonio, as well as several other men watched as Dick took a seat and proceeded to make every attempt at sliding the socks on.

"No, you need to roll them a bit, then work them onto your toes first," Antonio commanded, taking the socks from Dick as he was jamming his feet into them rather roughly.

"Here, allow me," Ricardo interjected as he moved in and took the socks from Antonio.

Kneeling, naked, before Dick, Ricardo expertly rolled each sock and worked them onto Dick's huge, slightly worn feet. He then proceeded to work the silky smooth socks up his hairy legs, until finally he snapped the tight bands around Dick's massive calves.

"There we go," Antonio commented as he enjoyed the sight of Ricardo in a submissive position at Dick's feet.

"Ok, now stand up. Next, we will get you into my undershirt and dress shirt," Ricardo directed Dick.

Dick stood now and waited for Ricardo to retrieve these items from the bar. He had to admit to himself that he was slowly, but surely, getting turned on by this scenario. At first he had thought that this would be a quick romp, but it was turning into something far more ritualistic and meaningful. He was really starting to appreciate this different way of dressing. There was something sexual about this, yet he couldn't place his finger on it just yet.

"Get those arms up boy!" Ricardo directed Dick once more, utilizing the guys own submissive term to refer to him.

"Yes Sir," Dick barked back with a smirk on his lips.

"That's it, put that bastard in his place," Buck added.

Slowly, and with great care Ricardo worked the pristine, white, cotton undershirt over Dick's upper body until his massive, ample pecs were encased in the fabric like a second skin. Next, Ricardo took his neatly pressed tuxedo shirt, with the lay-down collar, and helped Dick slide into it. The smooth fabric brushed over the hairs on each of his arms, causing them to tingle.

"Nice," Dick moaned, as a result of this new sensation. "We are far from done Richard," Ricardo prompted him, suddenly utilizing his formal name.

"So it seems Ric," Richard replied with an air of false self-importance in his voice.

Antonio and Vinny couldn't help but snicker to themselves at this sudden reversal of roles. Ricardo, now referred to as Ric, was suddenly in the role of the butch, commanding dominant, while Dick played the more submissive part as Richard, the soon-to-be formal stud.

"Very good boy," Ric noted, as he proceeded to apply each sparkling cufflink into the French cuffs of his shirt, which Richard had extended out for easy access.

Ric continued to work the matching set of shirt studs down along the front of the crisp, pleated shirt. With each stud the fabric became fuller and more tailored to Richard's immense body, his massive pecs and powerful arms filling the shirt to its limit. Richard reached up at this point and fastened the single pearl button at his throat. He loved the semi-claustrophobic feeling he was suddenly experiencing. The smooth, slightly cool fabric felt amazing against his body. The stiff cuffs at his wrists started to feel less constrictive and more comfortable – still tight, but more relaxed now.

"Ok, now for the challenging part," Ric noted, as he took the undone, silk bow tie in his hand. "We need that collar up boy," he continued, directing Richard to make way for the bow.

"Yes Sir," Richard replied.

With his massive paws he proceeded to work the stiff collar up, having to push aside his long, still slightly damp hair to allow Ric easy access. Ric stood behind Richard now and with expert hands flipped the soft, flaccid fabric into a sharp, perfectly styled, very erect bow.

"There. Perfect," Ric noted now as he stepped around Richard, working the collar down around the band of the tie that wrapped around Richard's thick neck.

"Lookin' good man," Buck commented now as he intently watched, mesmerized by the situation.

"Now, for the pants," Ric barked, as he extended his arm, directing Antonio to hand them to him.

Once in his grasp Ric proceeded to direct Richard into them, one foot at a time, until he was able to slide them up to his narrow waist and fasten them. However, the two men hit a roadblock, in the form of a massive, fully erect cock, as they attempted to fasten the pants closed.

"Hmm, well, now we have a problem," Ric noted, as he made every attempt to work the pants up and over and around the monstrous tool.

"I think, for now, that may have to hang through the opening," Antonio added, staring at the throbbing beast.

Realizing the same thing, at about the same time, Ric continued to work the pants to a point that he could clasp them closed, but the zipper would remain in the down position until further notice, allowing Dick's massive prick to swing freely.

"Ok, next come the suspenders, also known as braces in other countries such as England, for example," Ric instructed Richard.

Antonio was quick to hand these over and found enjoyment in watching his friend apply them to the blue-collar grunt. Snapping the single clasp to the rear, center of the tuxedo pants waistband, Ric now worked them over Richard's hulking shoulders, snapping each remaining strap to the front part of the waistband, just to the side of the pleated, mid-section of the tuxedo shirt.

"Excellent," Antonio commented.

"Lookin' sharp man," Vinny added, with a giddy, child-like tone in his voice.

"Turn around," Ric suddenly barked.

Richard did so and soon enough Ric and several of the other men had the perfect opportunity to check out his ample, muscular ass, now encased in very expensive, neatly tailored pants.

"Shoes!" Ric barked.

Antonio, foreseeing this command, was nearly in position with a pair of beautiful, imported, leather dress shoes. Richard slid his smooth, silky feet into each shoe and, once again, relished in the encapsulating sensation that occurred as his feet were placed in the most expensive set of shoes he had ever seen. After deftly tying the laces of each shoe Antonio directed Buck for a bar rag. With rag in hand, he proceeded to polish each shoe until there was an amazing shine to the leather. Standing and taking his place next to his friend the two men lingered on the sight before them. Regardless of how filthy the man was or how animalistic he seemed to be when they first met, both men inwardly acknowledged that Richard was looking extremely sexy suited up in Ricardo's tuxedo.

"Now, for the finishing touches," Ric muttered, as he directed Antonio to fetch the double-breasted tuxedo jacket from the bar.

"Turn once more," he continued, directing this statement toward Richard.

With his back to Ric, Richard extended his arms, slightly back, so that the jacket could be worked onto his arms and over his upper body. Once the jacket was in place upon Richard's shoulders Ric spun him around and proceeded to fasten the buttons at the front. After this was completed he continued to fuss with the silk pocket square, which had gone slightly limp while resting on the bar.

"A perfect fit," Ric barked to the crowd, who howled and barked in return, soaking in the image of their once rough and tough buddy, now suited to the nines. The fact that the man's enormous cock had to remain exposed only helped to heighten the eroticism of the image.

"Now it's your turn Vincenzo," Antonio barked to the man who seemed to be lost in the beautiful vision of his impeccably suited co-worker.

"Yes Sir," Vinny replied, enjoying the sound of his given name on the lips of his suddenly commanding game partner.

"Hold on," Ric suddenly barked. "Before we start with you, I think

Richard here needs to wear one more item."

Walking to the bar Ric picked up the pleated, silk cummerbund left behind on purpose.

"Turn around Richard," he commanded as he positioned himself behind the formally suited man, taking the cummerbund and using it as a blindfold instead of a waist sash.

"What's this for?" Richard questioned, slightly confused by this turn of events.

"I think I'd prefer Vincenzo's transformation to be a surprise to you," Ric replied.

"Perfect," Antonio added.

With that, the two men got to work suiting Richard's co-worker up in Antonio's gear. They followed the same process used on Richard and within minutes Vincenzo – as he was now being referred to – was suited to the nines. They even went as far as to slide him into Antonio's thick, cashmere coat, as well as finish him off with the silk scarf and leather gloves, once worn by the now stark naked man.

Richard, unable to view any of this couldn't help but fantasize in his mind what Vinny would look like in a tuxedo. He knew his buddy was handsome and the more he thought about it most of the crews he worked on referred to Vin as the 'Italian Stallion,' but he never thought he would have the chance to see him decked out in a tuxedo. Actually, he had never even thought of Vin in that context – as a suited stud – until now. What was happening to him? Where were these thoughts coming from? As he stood, waiting, and dreaming about his co-worker he could gauge how well the process of suiting Vin up was going by the hoots and hollers of the crowd.

"Yeah, baby, lookin' sharp man," he heard one drunken guy bellow.

"Smokin' hot," another added.

"I'll take a piece of that home," yet another barked.

"Ok men, calm down," Ric commanded as he gave Vincenzo a once over, making sure that every detail was exact. He then motioned to Antonio, directing him to dress as well.

The two formerly formal studs proceeded to collect the discarded pieces of the construction workers gear. Sliding into their filthy, worn garments was, at first, somewhat difficult for the two previously impeccably dressed men, but once they got past the sweat and stench they both started to get more than a little turned on by this change in dress.

Ric looked particularly hot in Richard's skin-tight jeans and equally tight wife beater, as well as his leather cowboy boots. Once he slid on the thick, leather, biker jacket he virtually blended in with the other guys in the bar, granted, his neatly groomed appearance still exposed him as a newbie to the underworld of leather.

Antonio – deciding to go by Tony now – followed Ric's lead and proceeded to dress in the remaining gear, up to and including the brown leather jacket that Vincenzo carried into the bar.

"Nice, very nice," Vincenzo commented to himself as he ran a gloved hand over the cashmere coat that hung from his shoulders and framed the muscle tight tuxedo, which he wore now with a bit of unexpected pride. "You guys look pretty fuckin' amazing too," he added as he gave both guys, now decked out in jeans and leather, the once over.

Richard stirred a bit, but remained silent, not wanting to disturb the three studs as they dressed, but by the way his massive cock was now throbbing and oozing pre-cum he couldn't control his mouth for long. He felt like he could erupt at any moment. He never fathomed how erotic wearing a tuxedo would be. The weight of it, the feel of it on his skin, the mere scent of it was driving him wild.

"Uh, guys?" he questioned them. "Did you forget about something?"

"Shut up bitch," Ric barked, as he strode over toward the blindfolded man, his cowboy boots clicking on the cement floor.

"Yeah," Tony now added, as he stood shoulder to shoulder with Ric, "we will tell you when we are ready for you."

"Yes Sir," Richard replied, standing more erect.

Ric and Tony proceeded to taunt, grope and caress Richard while he remained blindfolded and helpless. The two men, now leather studs, suddenly understood what it was like to take a more dominant role, while toying with a suited man. The feel of the neatly tailored tuxedo on this once filthy and vulgar grunt was amazing. The way it hugged his rock hard, work worn, muscular body was wonderful. What made it even more exciting to the two men was the extremely overpowering, masculine scent which he was so casually exuding.

The individual aromas of sweat, smoke and beer filled the air and mixed now with the strong cologne that still lingered from the two formally dressed men. Taking a good whiff, Ric and Tony soon found themselves lost in the moment. Ripping the blindfold off Richard, Ric turned the man to face his beautifully suited co-worker. He watched now – as Tony did – the reaction that formed on his slightly startled face.

"There. View your friend, Vincenzo," Tony barked, as he scanned the man's face and eyes for a register on what he was feeling.

It wasn't until a thick, copious stream of pre-cum slid out of Richard's painfully erect penis and struck the cement floor with a resounding splatter that Tony was able to tell if they had succeeded at causing the man extreme pleasure.

Richard's face remained focused and calm while his throbbing member twitched, pulsed and spewed. He was shocked at how gorgeous his buddy looked. He had always heard of people saying that their breath was taken away at the sight of something so unexpectedly beautiful, but he had never experienced the sensation himself – until now.

"Fuck," he was finally able to mutter.

"Exactly," Ric added. "That is exactly what we shall do. Here, now, for all to see."

Richard, unable at first to draw his eyes away from Vin, suddenly looked to Ric and found himself face to face with yet another unbelievable sight. There, before him, stood two of the hottest leather studs he had ever seen within the four walls of this bar. He found himself, once more, shocked by what he saw. Ric and Tony both stood now, leaning against the bar, staring Richard and Vincenzo down. There was a passionate, yet bestial glint in their eyes, which only heightened the eroticism of the situation.

"Are you serious?" Buck blurted out.

"Dead serious," Tony replied, as he groped his tightly packed crotch.

"Clear the way!" Ric barked as he motioned to the closest men. "We have some serious fucking to do with these two suited studs. Just look at them in their formal wear. Beautiful! It's almost a shame to mess with them."

"But, Ric, I wonder what made them come into this bar?" Tony questioned. "This isn't really their sort of place. Is it?"

"No, not at all. Suited men have no desire to play in such a filthy place," Ric replied with a sarcastic tone in his voice.

"Right. Suited men have no clue how to get rough, raw and passionate," Tony barked.

"No clue at all," Ric mockingly spat, as he walked up to Richard, grabbed him by his dangling, dripping cock, yanked him closer and proceeded to lock lips with him in an intense, passionate, tongue-filled kiss.

The men of the bar went wild now, screaming and shouting for more.

Tony watched as several men proceeded to clear a stage-like area, just to the right of the bar, preparing it for the four of them to play on. Ric noticed this as well as he withdrew himself from Richard's mouth.

"Excellent," he purred into the man's ear, "now we can really get down to business."

With that, Ric and Tony directed the two formal men toward the stage. At some point Tony had grabbed Ric's outerwear and was now taking the time to finish suiting Richard with it. As he slid the thick leather trench onto him Tony could tell that this was only enhancing the man's experience even more. Once he had the silk scarf and leather gloves on him, he motioned for him to get up on the stage with Vincenzo.

"There we go. Two fine examples of the male species," Ric barked as he took a seat on the edge of the stage. "Now gents, how should we go about doing this? Would the two of you like to have some time to play a bit before we join in or would you rather we just get this suit and leather orgy going full tilt?"

An awkward and somewhat alarming silence filled the room now, as the viewing audience waited, in anticipation, for an answer.

"Well?" Ric continued to probe. "What's it going to be?"

The two men, growing more and more comfortable in their formal attire by the minute admitted their desire for some group action.

"Come on up here and show us what ya got," Vincenzo replied as he ran a gloved hand over his beautiful new coat.

With that offer Ric and Tony did just that. Strutting up onto the stage the two newly transformed leather studs got to work.

"This one is mine," Ric barked, as he pointed to Vincenzo.

This selection caught Tony off guard, thinking that each of them would take on the man suited up in his own gear, but it appeared that that wasn't Ric's plan. His friend quickly moved into position closer to Vincenzo and proceeded to run a hand up and down the sleeve of his thick coat, moving ever so slowly into his personal space. The heat between them built, as he leaned in to kiss the man softly on his lips. Tony followed his friends lead and advanced on Richard, doing very much the same thing. Within minutes, the four men were lost in their duel, passionate embraces letting their mouths do most of the work.

Ric was the first one to pull away and proceed further along his quest for sexual fulfillment. Slowly, but firmly, he explored every facet of Vincenzo in his new gear. Doing so caused both men to moan ever so slightly. The feel of the different textures and fabrics drove Ric wild. He couldn't stop groping and caressing the man. As he ran his hand from the slightly rougher texture of the cashmere coat to the silky smooth fabric of the tux's lapels, Ric couldn't imagine a more erotic experience in the world. He had always loved suiting up – wearing his best gear out and about – but fondling this man here, in the company of others, was amazing. He glanced over at his partner in crime, only to see him enjoying Richard in very much the same way.

Tony, at first, was a tad bit rougher with Richard. As he ran his hands over the thick leather trench coat, he couldn't help but feel the desire to rip it off of him, exposing him in his tuxedo. He then had a mental image of him shredding the tuxedo to get to his muscular body. However, showing great control, he continued to gently caress and grope the man, until he finally gave into the throbbing, dripping beast that swung between the man's legs. Dangling out of the neatly tailored pants Richard's cock was a thing of beauty and Tony decided to appreciate it a bit more intimately.

Dropping to his knees now he proceeded to taunt and tease the man's bulbous, oozing cock head, which was now blazing a beautiful shade of red. As he ran his hot, very talented tongue around the fat tip Tony took the time to lap up every ounce of pre-cum that flowed from it. Moving down along the massive shaft, Tony continued working on the slick slab, flicking his tongue wildly, until it was time to take the monster into his hot mouth. Licking his thick lips he slowly drew Richard's engorged penis into his moist mouth. Inch by inch the throbbing rod slid further and further into Tony's mouth until it took a turn at his tonsils and slid further down his tight throat.

"Fuck!" Richard groaned.

"You keep saying that. Are you begging for it?" Ric mused, as he continued along his own erotic journey with Vincenzo.

"Shit," Richard moaned now as Tony expertly worked on his cock.

"I'm not sure about that. Not really into scat," Ric continued to toy with the man, as it appeared he was receiving the most amazing blowjob of his life.

Tony continued to suck the man's throbbing tool until he quickly pulled off – gasping for a bit of air – and stood, once again, only to kiss Richard deeply, feeding him his own sticky pre-cum. It was during the passion of this kiss that Richard found himself unable to hold back his animalistic tendencies. Grabbing the neckline to Tony's skin-tight shirt, he proceeded to shred it down the middle, exposing the rock hard pecs and abs held within. They glistened in the dim light, framed perfectly by the brown leather jacket that remained in place.

Grunting and moaning now, the two men started to dig into each other more ferociously.

Tony whipped the pure white, silk scarf from Richard's neck and spun him around, binding his wrists with it. He then turned him around once more and forced him to his knees. Once in position, Tony withdrew his own throbbing cock from his skin-tight jeans and began to dick whip Richard, until a thick stream of pre-cum was flowing from his piss slit.

"Yeah," Tony moaned. "Take that my formal bitch!"

Tony continued to strike Richard in the face, until, with one full thrust of his hips, he rammed his rock hard, dripping cock down the man's eager throat. Richard, in turn, drank in Tony's meat, drawing his pre-seed out.

Men barked and whistled as they watched their formerly dominant buddy get face fucked.

"Ya see men, a suit stud, as my buddy Tony here once was, can play rough too," Ric announced, before whispering something into Vincenzo's ear.

Watching the spectacle for several minutes more, Vincenzo finally moved into action, as directed by Ric. Strutting over to Richard, who continued to take Tony's powerful cock, Vincenzo proceeded to whip his own cock out and feed it to his co-worker.

Richard, gagging now, as his mouth became crammed with cock, suddenly felt a hand, much lower down, pushing aside his leather trench coat. The hand soon found its way toward the seat of his tuxedo pants. In an instant this same hand found its way along the seam of his pants, working its way up toward the waistband, until finally, with its five-fingered partner joining in, the two invaders were tugging and pulling, fighting with the expensive material, until, with one long audible rip, it gave. The crowd went wild once again as Ric proceeded to shred open Richard's neatly tailored pants, exposing his firm, lightly haired ass, with the seat of his bikini briefs riding up the man's ass crack.

"Look what we have here!" Ric barked, as he firmly slapped the exposed area and tugged on the bikini briefs, which were many sizes too small for the man.

With that, Ric yanked down his zipper, tugged out his cock and proceeded to slap the man's ass with it. Tony and Vincenzo continued to fuck Richard's face, as well as dick whip him, while the crowd cheered them on, eating up this erotic demonstration.

"Fuck him!" a drunken guy yelled.

"Take his muscular ass!" another barked.

"No!" Ric barked back, to the dismay of many, but then continued with a wicked smile on his lips, "Well, not without some protection that is."

Within seconds several dozen condoms littered the stage, tossed there by the way-too-eager crowd.

"Nice," Ric chuckled, "but I think just one will do for now," he concluded, bending to retrieve a single packet.

"Here, let me help you," Vincenzo suddenly addressed Ric as he withdrew his cock from Richard's gapping mouth.

Kneeling before Ric, Vincenzo took the condom in his gloved hand.

"I have a trick I do," he informed Ric as he ripped the wrapper off the rubber.

Placing the fresh rubber into his mouth Vincenzo grasped Ric's throbbing shaft and proceeded to roll it on, only using his tongue and lips to do so. Ric watched in amazement, wondering how a guy went about learning such a trick. He was sure that it took hours of practice. He quickly decided it was a hobby he could get into. Once wrapped in the condom Ric allowed Vincenzo the honor of directing his throbbing cock into Richard's ass. He watched as the tuxed stud pushed aside the seat of the bikini briefs and then guided him toward the dark, hairy hole found within. Slowly, inch by inch, Ric's dick slid into the firm, yet quivering ass of Vinny's co-worker.

Richard moaned now, as he had both of his holes filled with cock. His mind was whirling with erotic thoughts, as his body kicked into overdrive. Tony continued to thrust wildly, as Ric built up a rhythm of his own. The two men quickly found themselves repositioning Richard, after untying his bound wrists, so that he was on all fours now. This allowed both men easy access – one on each end. Vincenzo stood to the side for several minutes, enjoying the display. He soon found himself stroking, as he watched his buddy get dicked over.

"Damn," Vincenzo muttered, "I had no idea he was such a cock whore!"

"Yeah, right," Buck replied, with a chuckle as he watched the man eagerly take them both.

Richard's mind was reeling now as he felt the two thick, throbbing cocks attack his mouth and ass. He could only imagine what it looked like from the crowd's point of view – a tuxed stud worked over by two leather fuckers.

"Yeah," Ric moaned, as he thrust faster and faster into Richard's tight hole.

"Damn," Tony barked, as he worked himself deeper and deeper into Richard's throat.

The crowd continued to whistle and holler. A few of the intoxicated men started to work on their own throbbing cocks, stroking to the erotic scene. Vincenzo watched and stroked as well, feeling his load building and boiling inside of his full balls. The site of his buddy getting worked over was such a turn on that he wasn't sure he was going to be able to hold his load for much longer. He could feel it pulsing up his shaft, edging so close, but he did everything in his power to control its actual release.

Richard continued to work on the two cocks, one with his moist mouth and the other with his tight, dripping hole. As he did this he felt his body overheat inside of the tuxedo. He felt the sweat pour from his body and soak through the first few layers, causing them to cling to his muscular body – the tight cotton undershirt was first, quickly followed by the crisp dress shirt.

Tony and Ric continued to thrust deeper and deeper into Richard, until finally, Ric made a motion to his partner in crime that he was about to blow his load. Tony only responded with a nod, letting him know that he too was about to blast a hot one. Richard, expecting to feel their hot waves of seed at any moment was sorely mistaken, as both Ric and Tony withdrew themselves in unison. Collapsing to the floor Richard watched as the two men quickly approached his buddy.

Tony was quick to force Vincenzo to the floor, while Ric got into position, stripping the rubber from his throbbing cock. The two men stood over Vincenzo, who was staring up at them with a look of mild surprise on his handsome face and proceeded to release their hot loads. Blast after hot blast flew from the two pulsing cocks striking Vincenzo in the face, across his thick cashmere coat, onto his perfectly tied bow tie, across his neatly pressed dress shirt and even down upon his beautifully tailored dress pants. By the time the two men were done there were multiple rivers of seed flowing down upon Vincenzo's gear, as well as dripping from his lips and chin. Vincenzo, remaining in place and moaning a bit now felt the hot seed drip from his face. Within seconds he felt his own throbbing cock twitch and decided he couldn't hold the massive load found within any longer. Spewing like a fountain, his beautifully curved cock released its thick load up and all over his tuxedo clad body, drenching him even more.

"Damn," Tony grunted as he watched the abundant load splash upon Vincenzo and mix with the loads already there.

"I guess that curved cock comes in handy. When you're looking for a good cum bath that is," Ric added.

With that, Tony and Ric each took an end of Vincenzo's silk scarf and wiped their seed slick hands off on it.

"Ok, now back to Richard. I need several volunteers from the audience," Ric commanded.

Hands shot up all over the room, accompanied by grunts and hollers.

"Damn Ric, we may have a problem," Tony commented.

"Yeah, you may be right," Ric replied, as he eyed up the crowd.

"Let's just make this easy for everyone," Tony noted, as he went to Richard and pulled him up from the floor.

"Yeah, I think I see where you are going with this," Ric replied, as he stepped out of the way, allowing Tony to escort Richard off the stage and into the crowd.

The moment Richard stepped onto the main floor of the bar men were all over him – touching him, groping him, caressing him and then the comments came.

"Nice gear," one drunken guy barked as he ran a rough hand over Richard's leather trench coat.

"Very nice," another guy grunted, as he rubbed his exposed, pre-cum slick cock up and down the smooth surface.

Once one started to do this others followed until Richard felt several cocks rubbing against him. They continued to rub against his coat for several minutes, leaving pre-cum trails along the way, until they discovered the smooth, satin lining to the coat and proceeded to rub against that as well, staining it in pre-cum too. Then, they found his bare ass, still exposed from where Ric ripped the seat of his pants open and so they rubbed there too. As more and more men joined in Richard's still exposed, throbbing cock, continued to grow even more erect, oozing a river of pre-cum.

"Go for it men," Ric announced.

"Use that formal stud as he longs to be used," Tony added.

"Shit, what the hell am I waiting for?" Buck barked as he jumped the bar and made his way through the crowd straight for Richard.

The men continued to grope and caress and rub the tuxedo-clad man up and down, leaving pre-cum stains all over his gear. The feel of the fabrics such as leather and silk and satin drove them wild with passion and lust. Soon, men were stroking with parts of Richard's clothing, using the friction of the materials to get off.

To Richard, at first, it seemed as if he saw nothing but throbbing cocks all around him, but then, soon enough, it was eruptions of hot man seed that filled his view. One after another men blew their thick loads, coating him and his gear from head to toe.

Midway through the process a few of the men stripped off his leather trench coat so that they could soak down the tuxedo held within. Blast after blast of hot jizz splashed across the tuxedo jacket, the satin lapels and the silk pocket square. Then more cum came and struck his bow tie. Soon, even more seed was shot onto the lining of his tuxedo jacket. One man was even bold enough to remove Richard's dress shoes, using his silk-socked feet to get off. The punk proceeded to rub them all over his shaft until he shot a massive load, which flowed down his cock and onto the socks themselves.

Ric and Tony stood back now and watched as the men continued to buck, moan, grunt and howl, writhing in a massive pile, with a beautiful suited stud in the center of it all.

Within seconds of taking the last blast of hot seed Richard found himself pouring his own load, which was massive and unending, flowing from his enormous cock like a waterfall. The men stood back and watched as he dumped his load all over the leather trench coat that was now lying on the barroom floor.

"So, glad you came to the opera tonight?" Tony asked Ric with a wild smirk on his lips, as he continued to watch the men play.

"Uh, what opera?" Ric replied with a big shit grin on his face.

"You mean...?" Tony questioned Ric with a look of confusion on his face now.

"That's right man. You think I like the opera?" Ric barked back with a chuckle.

"So, this was all a set up?" Tony replied, as he began to put the pieces together.

"Well, you could call it that," Vincenzo added, as he stepped closer to the two men, "but my new boyfriend, Ricardo here, prefers to call his little game 'Bait and Switch' and, as luck would have it, you stumbled into the right place, at the right time – hook, line, and sinker."

Paying Dues

In the past Mark had often dreamed about living a life of wealth and comfort, but he began to realize, with great dismay – as the years piled up since his graduation – that working at a gym wasn't going to afford him that sort of lifestyle anytime soon. He slowly came to the understanding that his hopes and dreams were nothing more than unfulfilled fantasies, ones that would most likely fade away to faint memories as his continually sad and deprived life rolled along.

As of late he found himself sitting back at the front counter of the gym, watching the wealthy, younger members of the fitness club speed into the lot in their high-end sports cars, wearing the latest in fashion and flaunting the most expensive accessories a man could afford. He would continue to spy on them as they pranced around the workout floor – without an obvious care in the world - laughing and joking with each other as they passed their afternoons away pumping up their beautifully toned bodies. He often overheard them boasting about what they had purchased earlier in the day – some new garment or electronic gadget – and where they were headed for the evening – some swanky restaurant, nightclub or pub.

Don't these guys work for a living, he found himself thinking, for the millionth time, as he currently sat at his post logging members in and out, as well as handing them bottles of water and fresh towels on a particularly dull December day.

How do they afford such a lifestyle?

What did they do so right in their lives that they can just party and play all the time?

Why can't that be me?

These thoughts just kept eating away at his bitter, little mind as he updated gym memberships, entered new ones, and – to his slight satisfaction – mailed out overdue notices to the one or two tardy members who had failed to pay their dues.

Most of these punks are only a year or two older than I am!

Damn, some of them are even the same age, yet they have the power and wealth of guys twice our years.

How is this possible?

Again, his mind flooded with questions and complaints, inwardly lamenting over his lack of success and their overwhelming prosperity.

I can't take this anymore! It's just not fa...

But, it was in this moment, on this particular day – mid-thought – that Mark's life went from being simply dreadful to downright depressing. Forget about life not being fair, it was absolutely cruel at times.

There, before him, now stood the last two people in the world he had ever wanted to see again: Adam Chase and Paul Worthington III, two of the most detestable guys from his graduating class.

"Well, what do we have here?" Adam purred as he dropped his oversized leather gym bag and leaned on the counter, his strikingly handsome face now mere inches from Mark's own, with his thick cologne suddenly filling the air around them both.

"If it isn't Mr. Duncan," Paul added, as he too dropped his bag and stepped closer to get a better look.

The two of them filled Mark's line of sight in all their expensive, suited glory, towering over him in his somewhat feeble, seated position. The two looked like they had just stepped off a runway show for Abercrombie & Fitch and, just as back in school, appeared to be exact clones of each other. Their garments were flawless in every detail and tailored perfectly to their forms.

It made Mark sick to look at the two of them.

Both men were tall, built, and blonde and blue eyed, with neat, beautifully styled, thick hair and sparkling, bright eyes. They both had smooth, rich, tanned skin and their flashy smiles were perfectly straight and startlingly white. Your typical Ivy League studs.

Again, Mark wanted to puke.

Christ, he thought to himself, *just what I need. I should tell these two pricks to hit the road*, but "Uh, hi guys," was all he was able to muster on such short notice. He couldn't help but revert back to the nerdy, pushover kid they knew in school; regardless of the fact that physically he could match them muscle for muscle, ounce for ounce. Working at a gym did have its benefits after all.

"Yeah, hi," Adam mockingly replied, backing away now as he ran a hand over his perfectly knotted blue and white striped tie. "Now, listen, Matt..."

"My name is Mark," he was quick to correct.

"Uh, ok, anyway, listen up Mark. Paul and I would like to join this gym. We've heard that this place is one of the best in town," Adam commented. "But, listen, we hear it's also pretty pricey."

"Yeah, pricey," Paul added, as he too ran a hand over his own silk tie, "and we have better things to spend our money on."

"Now, being that we know each other, what do you say to a discount for your good, old classmates?" Adam added, with a bright smile.

"I'm not sure...," Mark began.

"Come on Matt...," Paul interrupted him, as he undid a polished button on his pinstriped suit, and removed a piece of lint from his lapel.

"It's Mark," he was quick to reply for the second time as he eyed up Paul.

"Huh?" Paul asked, now lost in the details of his beautifully tailored garment.

"My name is Mark, and, oh...Fuck it!" he suddenly found himself spewing at the two studs, tiring of having them anywhere near him.

"Excuse me?" Adam replied, with an 'I'm-going-to-ask-for-the-manager-soon' look on his handsome face.

"Sure, guys, whatever you want, it's yours," Mark spat, turning to the computer in disgust.

Quickly, and with little fanfare, Mark signed the two guys up and sent them on their way, rudely directing them to the locker room so that they could change out of their gorgeous suits and into their muscle-tight, gym gear.

With my luck I'll end up getting fired for giving them a fuckin' discount, Mark thought to himself, as he finished adding them to the system.

This is why you'll go nowhere in life!

This is why you will always be a servant to the rich assholes of this world!

Sitting at his station for several minutes more Mark suddenly glanced up at the clock to see that it was just about noon, which meant that his replacement would be in soon and he would be able to take his much needed break.

Within minutes he found himself in the employee lounge, which was located, oddly enough, right off the men's locker room.

Chomping down on his brown bag lunch Mark repeatedly played over his brief and frustrating encounter with Adam and Paul as he idly flipped through one of the many men's magazines left on the table before him.

Damn it, why was I so easy on them?

I really am a loser.

I have so little going for me in my life and here I had the perfect opportunity to reject the jerks that made my life a living hell in school...and I blew it!

It wasn't until Mark was just about finished with his break that his boss entered the lounge.

"Mark," Frank started, "we need to talk."

"Is everything ok?" Mark replied, suddenly feeling sick to his stomach, since it was so rare that his boss needed to speak to him. Perhaps it was the disappointed look on Frank's face that bothered Mark the most.

"Well, I wish I could say it was, but, well, it's not," Frank replied, running a massive hand through his spiky, blonde-brown hair.

"What's wrong?" Mark muttered.

"I just reviewed today's membership log and I see that you keyed two of our newest members in with a deep discount fee. Care to explain this?" he asked, crossing his massive arms over his equally massive chest.

Mark suddenly felt the room spin, as his lunch began to crawl back up his throat. Stunned into silence he was unable to come up with a quick or worthy reply. Inwardly he was cursing himself for being so stupid, mentally beating himself up. Then, suddenly, to his surprise, he envisioned a set of 100lb. weights falling on Adam and Paul's heads as they worked out in the next room. For some reason this brought him much joy, but, sadly, still no response.

"I see," his boss noted, with a bit of grief in his voice, as Mark failed to defend himself. "Well, since this is your first screw-up I'm putting you on locker and bathroom duty until further notice. When you get back from your break head straight there and make sure that both areas are sparkling by the end of your shift. Understood?"

"Yes," Mark muttered, hanging his head now.

"Good," Frank replied, as he left the lounge, giving Mark a firm squeeze on his left shoulder before he departed.

Damn, why am I so stupid? Even Frank hates me now!

Dragging himself from his seat Mark preceded out of the lounge and directly into the men's locker room. Thankfully it was devoid of members. However, he was instantly struck by the heady odor of masculinity that clung to every object in the room. No matter how hard the staff cleaned, there was always this ever-present aroma and, oddly enough, Mark was one of the few to find it somewhat intoxicating, arousing even. If only he was able to tolerate the men who created such a powerful aphrodisiac.

Christ, and now I get to clean up after all of these rich assholes, he thought with a sneer on his lips. *How perfect. I really hope those two jerks are gone.*

Then, as if a sign from above or, more appropriately, a slap in the face, he noticed Adam's gym bag, which was sitting on the top of the last row of lockers.

Damn. I knew I couldn't be that lucky.

Slowly walking the line of lockers, Mark approached Adam's leather bag, which, he could now see was placed right next to Paul's.

I should take them both down and piss in each one, he suddenly thought with a smile on his face. *Although, that would just get me in even more trouble. God knows Frank has enough on his plate already.*

Readying himself for yet another confrontation with the two jerks he quickly got to cleaning the locker room and then the bathroom. It wasn't until about an hour later, as well as several filthy toilets and urinals, that he noticed that Adam and Paul's bags were still sitting in the same spot.

Exiting the room Mark circled the workout floor, only to find no trace of either guy.

Heading to Frank's office he gently knocked and waited for a reply before entering.

"Come in," his boss replied.

For the second time in one day Mark felt his lunch make its way up his throat and almost out of his mouth. There, before him, stood not only his boss, but a police officer as well.

Shit. Is Frank actually going to have me arrested for giving them a stupid discount? This is crazy!

"Mark, please, come in. I was just about to call for you," Frank motioned at him with a broad hand and a very serious look on his face.

"Sure," Mark replied, unable to take his eyes off the uniformed officer, whom, he decided didn't need the gun at this belt, since his exposed arms were enough to scare any person into submission.

"It appears that your two friends were caught up in a bit of trouble earlier today and, so, as it just happens, because you were so nice to allow them to join our club their credit cards flagged in the main network and Officer Jeff Michaels here was able to trace them. An apprehension was made about 20 minutes ago."

Stunned, Mark felt his heart skip a beat.

Fuck yeah! Take that, you stupid bitches!

"I can see from the look on your face that there is no love lost over their capture. So, as a reward, you can take the officer back to their belongings and help him dispose of them accordingly," Frank noted now, as he motioned for Mark to escort the uniformed man back to the locker room.

"Yes," Mark beamed.

With that, he practically jogged out of the office, almost leaving the officer behind.

"Wait up, boy," Officer Michaels called to Mark, swiftly catching up with him as he took several broad steps down the hallway toward the eager, young attendant.

"Oh, sorry," Mark replied, pausing at the door.

"Can I ask you something?" Michaels questioned.

"Sure," Mark beamed again, looking up at the man, who was easily several inches taller.

"Did you know Mr. Chase and Mr. Worthington very well?"

"I went to school with them," Mark blandly replied, meeting the man's steady gaze.

"Ah, and let me guess, the two of them were your typical class jocks, while you were, well...," the officer's words trailed off now.

"Uh, yeah, as my boss already stated...no love is lost here over their sudden departure," Mark replied with a big shit eating grin.

"Understood. Now, can you show me where their belongings are? Michaels prompted Mark.

"Certainly," Mark replied, leading him to the last row of lockers and pointing out their bags, as well as the two lockers below.

"No locks?" Michaels questioned. "They were either far too cocky or just too stupid."

"Well, probably a little of both, they did use their credit cards when clearly they should have avoided doing that," Mark was quick to add.

"Listen, if I am right, I think what we'll find in one of these two bags will be enough evidence to put them away for several years. So, what do you say we pretend the other bag got a little lost in the shuffle?"

Mark, confused by this sudden turn of events quietly stood by as Officer Michaels popped both of the lockers open.

"As for these," he noted, with a smile and a gloved hand, the two designer suits, "you can have them as well."

"Really?" Mark replied, with a bit of hesitation in his voice.

"Yeah, I don't see why you can't be rewarded for helping us capture these two losers," Michaels replied with a smile on his rugged face. "Besides, it looks like you've done some lifting in your days to catch up with these two ex-jocks. I bet you'll fit these suits as perfectly as they once did."

"That's kind of you to say, but...," Mark let his words trail away now, suddenly feeling a bit self-conscious.

"I'm just calling it as I see it," Michaels replied, eyeing Mark up and down now. "Here, how about this. I'll let you keep them, if you can show me how one looks on you. If it fits, it's yours. If it doesn't I take them back to the station."

"Uh, I guess that sounds like a pretty good deal," Mark eagerly replied, suddenly willing to go along with the cop and his plan.

"Good, now, how about you get out of those work clothes and into a designer suit?" Michaels noted as he took a seat on the wooden bench that ran the length of the lockers.

"Ok, but, I'm not sure...," Mark looked to the door of the room.

"Oh, if you're worried about your muscle-headed boss leave him to me," Michaels replied, motioning to the closest locker and suit. "Now, suit up."

Hesitating for only a brief minute Mark began to strip out of his gym uniform. This included: a pair of slightly worn, black sweatpants, a rather bulky, white sweatshirt and a pair of black, workout sneakers. Under this all, he had on a brand new white jockstrap, a crisp, cotton tank top and a pair of thick, white gym socks.

Standing now in only his socks and strap, Mark looked to Officer Michaels for what to do next, feeling rather lost in the art of dressing in a suit.

"Well, first of all, let me say – daaaamn boy! You've managed to hide one hell of a tight body under all that shitty gym gear," he noted, with a broad smile on his full lips, which caused his thick mustache to bristle a bit, as his eyes drifted down to the two firm globes that rested perfectly on the straps of Mark's jock. "Now, let's see what the guys left behind for you, because I'm thinking there just may be a new pair of shorts and socks waiting for you in one of these lockers. Although, I must admit, I wouldn't mind if you left that jock on. Damn."

Mark, somewhat embarrassed now, was quick to reach into the first locker, and after fumbling around a bit, turned up with a pair of black, silk boxers.

"Hmm, how about what's behind door number two?" Michaels jokingly commented, eyeing up the delicate silk boxers.

Reaching into the second locker Mark quickly pulled out a pair of white, cotton boxer briefs.

"I guess I can live with those. Put them on," the officer directed Mark.

Turning away now Mark slid off his jock and proceeded to work the boxer briefs onto his body. They felt cool and slightly more confining than his previous underwear – although he really liked the texture of the cotton upon his skin.

"Nice. Now, how about some more appropriate socks?" the officer noted, eyeing up Mark's thick, white ones.

Rooting around Mark was quick to withdraw a pair of black, silk, over the calf socks.

"Excellent," Michaels noted. "You may want to take a seat when you put those on."

Following these orders Mark did just that.

Sitting mere inches from the cop Mark worked off his thick socks and slowly slid the silky, smooth footwear over his bare feet.

Wow, he thought to himself, *these feel amazing!*

Wiggling his toes a bit and relishing the newfound sensation Mark started to suddenly feel a bit more comfortable about suiting up in clothing that was not his own.

This is it man! You are getting a taste of what it is like to be rich and powerful! It's like a dream come true.

Jumping to his feet now Mark nearly stumbled over the officer to get back to the locker that contained the rest of the suit.

"Whoa, slow down boy. There's no need to rush into this," Officer Michaels noted as he drank in the image of the nearly naked, muscular kid before him. "Garments such as these need to be treated with respect and great care."

"Ok," Mark replied, as he slowed in his motions, gently taking the pieces of the suit from the locker.

He was amazed at the weight of it. While it had the appearance of being heavy, it was in reality rather light and airy in his hands. To Mark this meant only one thing – it must have cost a fortune!

"Ok, well, first you need an undershirt as well as a dress shirt," Michaels informed Mark.

Standing, the officer reached into the locker himself and withdrew a solid, blue dress shirt. As he turned it over in his hands he could now make out the double-wide, white, French cuffs, as well as the stiff, button down, contrasting white collar.

"Nice," he muttered to himself as he held it in one gloved hand while reaching into the locker once more to retrieve the undershirt with the other. "Here," he noted, as he handed the last item to Mark.

Mark, taking the undershirt in his hands slid it over his head and pulled it down around his upper body. It stretched and expanded over his thick, toned muscles, hugging him like a second skin. His oversized, brown nips were now reduced to simple bumps under the surface of the smooth, cool shirt.

"Turn around," Michaels instructed him now as he helped him slide into the tailored dress shirt. "I think this is going to fit perfectly."

With his back to the officer, he maneuvered his arms so that they could easily slide into the garment. As they did, the hairs on his arms rose and tingled. It was a wonderful sensation how the expensive fabric slid and ran all over his skin, encasing his upper body flawlessly.

"There, see, I knew it would fit you well," the cop noted as he turned back to the locker to gather up the chunky, gold, block-shaped cufflinks that were sitting on the shelf inside. "You put these in the cuffs," he continued to instruct the kid, who seemed to know nothing about dressing like a real man since the expression on his face was more blank than knowing.

"Ah, I always wondered about those," Mark replied, confirming the officer's thoughts.

Damn, I sound like such an idiot. I should know better than this! No wonder I'm such a low man on the totem pole of life.

"Correct," Michaels assured Mark, as he supervised the placement of the links. "Fold the cuffs back and slide those babies through, then twist them so they stay in place. Now, allow me to button you up."

Officer Michaels stepped closer to the kid and reached forward. With his two, massive, leather-clad paws, he nimbly fastened the buttons up the front of the shirt until each one was snuggly in place, drawing the fabric of the shirt tighter around Mark's torso.

Mark inhaled deeply and held his breath as he allowed the cop to fuss with the shirt. Having the man invade his personal space was alarming and, yet, enjoyable all at the same time.

Damn this guy is aggressive and fuckin' huge too! He could probably snap my neck like a twig if he wanted to.

"There, all secure. Now, for the pants," Michaels noted, as he took a step back and looked the boy over.

Turning, Mark slid the pants of the dark blue suit from the bench where he had placed them earlier. Working his feet into the leg openings he pulled them up and fastened them at his narrow waist, only after tucking in his shirt. The feeling of the cool, silk lining which ran along the inside of each leg to just about his knees was delicious. It reminded him of sliding into a swimming pool on a warm summer day, letting the fresh water wash over his skin.

"Perfect," the cop noted as he slid a black, snakeskin belt with a gold buckle from the locker. "Here, you probably don't need this, but it will dress up the suit nicely."

Taking the item from Michaels, Mark worked it around his waist and fastened it, inwardly agreeing that it was more decorative than functional.

"Now, I usually like to slide my shoes on next, but we can work on the tie, if you would like."

"Sure," Mark replied. "If that works for you it's fine with me."

Stepping back Officer Michaels removed the matching, black, snakeskin shoes from the bottom of the locker. Turning, he knelt at Mark's feet and helped him work his silk socked feet into each shoe.

"Wow. Who would have guessed that Adam and I had the same size feet," Mark replied. "His always looked bigger than mine."

"Well, Mark, it's all in how you carry yourself," Officer Michaels encouraged the kid. "If you can talk the talk, you can walk the walk. Just don't act like too much of an asshole to those around you. Always remember, regardless of what people say – it's the man that makes the clothes, not the other way around. Although, I must admit, sharp clothes such as these do help to make a good first impression."

"Yes," Mark simply replied, as he wiggled his toes around the inside of the comfortable, highly polished shoes.

"Now, shall we train you in the art of the tie?"

"Yes," Mark replied, eager now to add the finishing touches to his new look.

"Well, there are several knots that I can show you, but, I think for now, we will whip this blue and white striped baby into a neat, double Windsor," Michaels noted as he withdrew the silk tie from the locker and approached Mark. "Collar up," the cop was quick to add as he moved behind him.

Working the stiff collar to his shirt up Mark inhaled deeply and allowed his personal space to be invaded once more. The officer's thick arms were soon brushing against his shoulders as well as the sides of his neck as he fussed with the silk fabric, working it into the perfect knot. The close proximity of their bodies was titillating. Yet, it wasn't until Mark felt the officer's ample bulge against his firm suited ass that he realized the man was thoroughly enjoying the situation too. With every move Michaels made his fully packed crotch brushed against his rear. Over and over the officer continued to rub his uniform-clad erection against Mark's sleek trousers, until he finally completed the task at hand.

"Ok, there we go. You're almost finished," the cop informed the kid as he stepped around to the front and buttoned the collar over the band of the tie. "The last piece of the puzzle is the suit jacket and trust me when I say if you thought the rest made you feel good and look great, just wait until you have that particular item draped over your body."

Taking the jacket into his hands Michaels stepped behind Mark once again and just as with the dress shirt worked the coat up along his arms until the neatly tailored collar brushed along the back of his neck. Once again, for only an instant, Mark had the pleasure of feeling the officer's manhood press against his suited ass. However, Mark quickly became distracted by the sensation of the silk lining running along the material of his shirt, confining his body even more. It was captivating and caused a stirring in his briefs.

"Everything ok Mark?" Officer Michaels questioned the somewhat overcome kid.

I couldn't be better fucker, was what he thought, but, "Uh, yeah," was all that came out of his slightly parted lips as he brushed a hand over his own crotch, attempting to calm himself down. There was no need for both of them to be so obvious in their arousal...was there?

"Well, Mr. Duncan, I'm guessing you will end up with this suit after all. It fits you beautifully."

"Thanks," Mark replied as he slowly approached the full-length mirror located between the lockers and bathroom, attempting to put a little distance between the two of them.

Approaching his reflection, Mark was lost for words, and found himself gasping to catch his breath. He looked...

Amazing, was all he could muster in his overwhelmed mind.

He stood for several minutes looking himself over, appreciating every detail of the garment that fit him as if it were tailored just for him and not some snot-nosed asshole. Officer Michaels silently watched from a distance with a smile on his face until he felt the sudden urge to jot a note in his pad that he kept handy on his thick utility belt.

"Well," Michaels commented, after putting his pad and pen away, "I think my work is done. I'm going to take this bag down to the office while you go off and enjoy your new found riches. Speaking of which, don't forget your other suit, as well as your bag. I think you'll be pleasantly surprised what you discover inside. However," he concluded, as he picked up Mark's discarded jockstrap, "this is coming with me."

Mark smiled to himself at the gesture but soon became distracted by the thoughts racing around in his head.

"Officer Michaels, please, be honest, are you sure this is ok?" Mark questioned, suddenly wondering if he would be the next one taken off to jail for agreeing to this quickly developing and rather questionable situation.

"Boy, trust me, they won't miss a thing. As I already stated, these items are your reward for helping us apprehend two very nasty fuckers," Michaels spat now with a grim look on his face as he shouldered the leather bag that was once in his hand and made his way for the door.

"Well, Sir, if you find that you need these items back just say the word, I will return them," Mark muttered as he continued to run his eyes over the gorgeous garment, gingerly caressing the material.

"Something tells me I couldn't rip that suit out of your clutches if I wanted to," Michaels noted, as he looked Mark over from head to toe.

"Well, perhaps we could test that theory out one day soon," Mark replied, with a surprisingly mischievous sparkle in his eyes and swagger in his walk. "Repeatedly, until I beg for you to stop, Sir."

"Damn. I put you in a suit for a minute and you suddenly turn into a flirtatious, twisted pervert. I think I've created a monster," Michaels jokingly replied, with a broad smile on his face.

"No, you've made yourself a Master and I'm more than willing to be your suited servant," Mark replied, with an equally broad smile.

"Well, I will have to take that into consideration, but for now I need to get my ass back to work and you need to secure your valuables," Officer Michaels commanded as he suddenly turned and left the room.

And what a fine ass it is, Mark thought to himself as he approached the leather bag that the cop left behind.

Placing a hand on the zipper he pulled it across the top of the bag and for the third or fourth time in one day he found his heart racing nearly out of control. There, before him, in neat, crisp packs were bundles and bundles of bills – green bills, with rather impressive numbers on them.

Holy crap! I'm rich! Mark inwardly screamed, but quickly recovered himself, as he reached for the hand-written note sitting next to the bag.

Mark,

> *You've paid your dues in life and now it's time for life to give you a little bit back in return.*

> *Don't spend it all in one place, at one time. The serial numbers can be traced.*

> *I'll be watching and waiting for you.*
> *Stay out of trouble boy,*

> > > > *Jeff – a fellow, former nerd*

With a smile and a newfound purpose in life Mark not only marched out of the locker room – with bag in hand and the second suit folded over his arm – but he continued right through the front doors of the gym and out into the world. A new world...one that would soon show him the respect he so longed for and desired, in his gorgeous, newly acquired designer suit.

Quartet

As Marco approached the barbershop, he took a moment to glance at his reflection in the oversized, front window. He wasn't really sure about heading inside the shop, but his partner had been complaining lately about the hairs left all over the bathroom so he felt obligated to do something about his somewhat shaggy appearance. His full head of thick, wavy, black hair was growing a bit long these days, especially in the back. Marco personally thought the look was 'in,' but clearly his partner thought differently. Taking another objective look, a shave would be in order as well, as he ran a masculine hand over his shadowed jaw.

Standing now, checking himself out in the window, he took note of how sharp he currently looked in his black, pinstriped suit and thick, cashmere overcoat, regardless of his unshorn look. The fit and cut of both were perfect, which he expected, since he had them specifically tailored to meet his needs.

Having a compact, football-player type body often led to problems when purchasing clothing. The tailor, at his favorite suit shop, usually had to spend many an hour adjusting his suits so that they fit beautifully. His tailor also had to special order Marco's overcoats, which often required a shorter length, but a much broader shoulder, as well as a fuller chest. At 5'8" and 220 lbs., Marco was built like a bull – solid, muscular and stocky.

He was currently wearing his favorite three-button suit made of a heavy, woven silk. Under the suit, he had on a rich, lilac-colored dress shirt with stiff French cuffs and a wide, cutaway collar. His tie was a beautiful combination of black, gold, purple and white stripes, perfectly knotted at his throat, and made from the most amazingly soft silk. On his feet, he wore a pair of classic, lace-up Oxfords, in black, which matched his sheer, over the calf, dress socks.

He had to admit to himself, he was looking and feeling rather dashing. In particular, he really enjoyed the texture of his silk tie, which felt like butter against his skin each time he fussed with it.

Taking one more look at himself, he ran a hand through his thick hair, checked his tie once more, and then proceeded into the barbershop.

"Marco!" his barber called, as he walked through the front door, setting off the small, old-fashioned bell attached to the doorframe.

"Alex," Marco replied, as he slid out of his coat and handed it to the rather young, cute receptionist sitting at the counter near the entrance.

"Let me finish with my good friend Perry here and after that I shall get to work on you," Alex noted with a bright smile, as he turned back to his current customer.

Marco proceeded to take a seat along the wall in one of the many leather chairs found there. The cute assistant, dressed in a pair of tight, black, flat-front trousers and an equally tight, button down dress shirt in a striking, jade green was quickly at his side offering him a magazine and a drink.

"I'm good," Marco replied with a polite smile and a wave of his hand.

"Yes Sir," the assistant chirped, as he sauntered back toward the front counter.

Marco often enjoyed just sitting, waiting and watching Alex work, with little to distract him.

Alex was the type of man Marco considered to be one of those rare individuals who was breathtakingly handsome, but, oddly enough, severely humble at the same time. He was in his late thirties; this much Marco knew to be true. He had also once worked as a model for several years for one of the most successful fashion houses in the city. And from his current appearance he still carried and presented himself like a professional, who could easily jump back into the business in a heartbeat.

At 6'3" and 225lbs., Alex was statuesque, although, having packed on a few more layers of muscle since his days on the runway; he had a much more masculine appearance now than the slightly leaner, pretty-boy look preferred by designers. His thick, tightly curled, blond-brown hair was styled beautifully – as expected – and his piercing, pale-green eyes stood out from his flawless, deep tanned skin. He had the look of a Greek deity, fresh off Mount Olympus, with his strong, powerful profile.

As Marco watched the man work, trimming and styling away, he quickly took inventory of his clothing.

Dressed in a pair of beautifully tailored, black, pinstripe pants, Alex moved with the comfort and ease of a man accustomed to fine garments. Upon his toned upper body, he wore a fitted, crisp, white dress shirt, with the sleeves neatly rolled up to reveal his slightly hairy, muscular forearms. Over this, he wore a matching, black, pinstripe vest, with a striking back panel done in an ultra-shiny silk. He had several of the polished buttons undone on the vest, just as he had the first two buttons of his shirt open, which gave him a relaxed, casual look. Around his neck, he wore a loosely done, yet well-knotted, silk tie, which matched the color of his assistant's dress shirt. Lastly, upon his feet, he had on a pair of classy, retro, black and white wingtips, which clicked on the tiled floor as he moved.

"Marco, have you ever met my friend Perry here?" Alex suddenly called out, bringing Marco out of his trance.

"No," Marco simply replied.

"Well, I think the two of you would really hit it off," Alex continued, as he finished running a brush over Perry's broad shoulders, just to ensure that any random clippings were whisked away.

As the man stepped from the chair, he turned and faced Marco now, extending a well manicured hand toward him.

"Perry Richards," the freshly groomed, blonde-haired gentleman introduced himself now.

"Marco Casari," he replied, as he extended a hand.

"Nice to meet you," Perry replied, giving Marco the once over.

"Likewise," Marco returned, eyeing Perry up as well, locking eyes with him for a moment, as the handshake between them lingered for a few seconds longer than a traditional exchange.

"Perry here is one of the most creative, intelligent men I know, excluding you, of course," Alex commented now, as he finished cleaning off the barber chair before him.

"Well, I don't know about that...," Perry noted, as he reached for his three-quarter length leather jacket, which was brought to him by the blonde assistant.

"Leaving already?" Marco questioned the man, as he watched him slide into his coat.

"Actually, now that I think about it...no," Perry replied, sliding his coat off and handing it back to the very attentive assistant. "I think my shoes need a shine before I go."

"Excellent," Alex replied, as he motioned for his assistant to set Perry up for a complete shine. "As for you Marco, have a seat," he motioned now to the chair before him.

"Billy, make sure you give Perry the full treatment," Alex directed his assistant, with a wink and a nod, as he slid Marco's suit jacket off.

"Yes Sir," Billy replied, as he directed Perry to the shoe shining station located in the rear of the shop.

"He's a good kid," Alex commented to Marco now, as he hung the jacket, "He may not be the sharpest scissor in the drawer, but still, he's a good kid."

"Easy on the eyes too," Marco added, as he slid into the red, leather, swiveling barber's chair.

"Yes, that's very true, my friend," Alex replied, as he ran a hand over his tools on the counter before him.

"Cute ass too," Marco threw in now, as he leaned a bit back in his chair to catch a view of Billy as he knelt before Perry, taking the man's shoe into his hand and placing it on the slender metal footrest before him.

"Ok, enough about the boy and more about you. What are we doing for you today?" Alex spoke, as he took his position behind the chair.

"Well, a cut and a shave to start," Marco replied, as he ran a hand through his slightly unkempt hair and then over his jaw.

"I see. Is your man giving you a hard time again?" Alex replied, with a playful expression on his handsome face.

"Yes. I guess he is," Marco replied, using the mirror before him to make eye contact with his friend.

"Well, we can't have that," Alex insisted, as he leaned in now to adjust Marco's tie and shirt collar so that they would not hinder his work.

This part of the process always drove Marco wild. He loved how commanding Alex was in the situation, and how vulnerable he felt in return. He loved the sensation that washed over him as Alex moved into his personal space.

In a way, it was all very sensual to Marco and he relished the experience to the limit.

As Alex leaned in, from behind, and took a firm hold of Marco's beautifully knotted silk tie, he could feel the hairs on the barber's muscular forearms brush against his neck. He watched, in the reflection of the mirror, as Alex carelessly tugged and yanked on the once perfectly knotted silk tie, which had taken him, that morning, many minutes to get just so. It didn't seem to matter to the barber, who dove in without any hesitation, eager to get the job done. He continued to work on it, rather roughly, undoing the knot just enough to get to the top buttons of Marco's dress shirt.

"Jeez Marco, you are bound up like Fort Knox here," Alex commented, as he continued to work on the top two polished buttons of Marco's lilac-colored shirt, shoving the silk tie out of the way.

Marco didn't comment and, instead, just sat back in the chair, letting Alex defile his impeccable appearance. He took a certain perverse pleasure in being handled this way, especially by such a handsome man. He loved to watch, helplessly, as Alex undid him – both physically and, secretly, emotionally.

"There we go," Alex finally stated once he had the shirt and tie adequately loosened.

"Thank you Alex," Marco replied, drawing in a breath.

"Ok, now, let's make sure we don't mess you up anymore than we need to," Alex noted with a mischievous grin, as he took one of his long, silken drapes and covered Marco with it, tucking it into his stiff, slightly open collar. He then brought a small, white, cotton towel and tucked that in along Marco's neckline as well.

"In your hands, I would never consider myself a mess," Marco half-heartedly joked, as he tugged on the drape, from below, to ensure that he was completely covered.

"Oh, really," Alex replied now with a wicked smile, as he stepped around the chair, heading for the counter and his tools.

"Well...," Marco chuckled, more to himself than to the man before him.

"Ok. Let's see what's going on with this head of yours," Alex suddenly noted, as he casually came at Marco with a comb.

Drawing the comb through Marco's thick hair, Alex placed a firm hand along the side of his neck so that his head wouldn't jerk about too much. The sensation of the comb being drawn through his locks always made Marco's scalp tingle. The feeling of the barber's hand on his neck, always made something else twitch and tingle too, but that was well concealed by the silk drape.

"Marco, your head of hair is one of my favorites to work on. Have I ever told you that?" Alex commented, as he continued to draw the comb through.

"No. I don't think you have," Marco replied, waiting for a further explanation as to why this was the case.

"It's just so thick, yet manageable. It lies beautifully and, surprisingly, I still don't see a grey among the jet," Alex continued, as he expertly worked the comb. "How old are you again?"

"36," Marco replied, with a slightly sheepish grin.

"Ah, just about my age and not a grey to be seen for miles. You are damn lucky my friend," Alex continued, as he fussed a bit more with his bare hands now and less with the actual comb.

Marco drew in a long breath to calm himself, as he felt the barber's masculine hands work through his hair. His nimble fingers ran through Marco's generous locks, gently caressing the surface of his scalp along the way. Alex had a subtle way of doing this without it seeming too personal.

"Ok, well, it appears that we can probably take a good inch off," Alex informed Marco, as he held the tips of dark hair between his fingers, "maybe two."

"That sounds good," Marco lazily replied, as he continued to enjoy the sensation of Alex's fingers in his hair.

Alex now grabbed a spray bottle, filled with warm water, and ran it around Marco's head, shielding his eyes along the way, as he drenched the thick hairs down. Then, once again, he ran a nimble hand through Marco's now damp hair, re-measuring the length.

"Yes. We will probably go with almost two inches off," Alex noted.

Once content with the level of dampness, and the decision on length, he moved into action, grabbing a pair of scissors and working his comb through with great skill.

SNIP. SNIP. SNIP.

He skillfully worked his tools around Marco's head.

SNIP. SNIP. SNIP.

He continued to run his fingers through his hair, tugging and twisting it, as he snipped away.

Marco watched in the mirror, as Alex became intense in not only the expression on his handsome face, but in the movements of his casually suited body. There was a sense of severe focus now, almost as if he had slipped into a zone. He was clearly working his magic. The silence that occurred now, between the two men, was expected, and not awkward in the least.

Marco remained focused on Alex for several minutes more until he suddenly realized he was able to catch a glimpse of Perry and Billy in the mirror. It appeared that Billy was nearly finished with the man's first shoe and was about to make a move toward the other foot. Marco watched as Perry stared down upon Billy, keeping a close eye on the boy as he finished the initial shining of his left shoe. He was certain that he caught a rather amused expression on Perry's face or...was that a look of *pleasure* he was seeing?

Focusing his attention on the man now, Marco was certain that he was witnessing a rather personal exchange occur between the two men. The way that Billy held the man's foot and glanced up, almost seductively, to make eye contact with Perry wasn't what Marco would have considered a normal shoe shining practice. Marco soon noticed that Billy was also slowly tracing a finger along the rim of the leather shoe, right at the spot where Perry's socked foot was partially exposed.

He continued to watch as Perry licked his lips a bit, shifted in his seat and adjusted his pants. Something forbidden was going on back there and Marco was somewhat surprised that the two men would take such a public risk. Although, truth told, the thoughts that were racing through his own mind were not that innocent either.

As he turned his attention back to Alex, he couldn't help but think about how amazing it would be to have this man use his skilled hands below the neck, as well as below the belt. His hands felt incredible as they worked their way through his hair. The sound of the scissors clicking away filled his ears and became a sort of mantra, as Alex continued to work wonders on his shaggy mop.

Within a matter of minutes, Alex had him trimmed up beautifully, but not before he proceeded to lean in and against Marco, occasionally brushing his suited crotch against his knee.

"Well now, how does that look?" he questioned Marco, as he continued to primp and fuss, running his hands – which had a styling gel smeared on them now – through his neat hair.

Marco looked at his reflection in the mirror and smiled. Once again, he looked much more civilized with a very handsome head of hair. His partner would be happy to see this.

"Yes. It's perfect," Marco replied, as he tilted and twisted his head to get a better view.

Alex held a mirror to the rear of Marco's head to give him an even better opportunity to inspect the cut.

"Very nice," Marco smiled, as he brought one of his hands out from under the drape and fussed with it himself.

"Now, I believe you are in need of a shave," Alex noted, as he turned toward the counter to return his comb and scissor, and retrieve his shaving equipment.

"Yes, that would be great," Marco replied, as he adjusted himself in the chair, once again glancing toward the naughty duo in the rear of the shop.

Once more, his attention was drawn to Perry who was watching the boy with an eager, lustful eye. The boy, still on his knees, now had Perry's left shoe off and was intently massaging his socked foot. Perry shut his eyes and let his head fall back, as he allowed the boy to do his work. Slowly, Billy brought the socked foot toward his face and right to his lips. He began to nuzzle and kiss the man's silk encased foot, working his mouth and tongue all over it from toe to heel.

Marco drew his gaze away, feeling as if he was suddenly intruding upon them. Returning his attention to Alex, he soon realized that the man was patiently waiting for him.

"Enjoying the show?" Alex questioned, as he took his freshly made bowl of shaving cream in hand and dropped the large brush, he held in his other hand, into it.

"I, uh, well...," Marco stumbled over his words.

"I'm not blind Marco," Alex whispered, "I can see them back there as well, but as long as the two of them are not hurting anyone, why interrupt them?"

Marco, slightly surprised by this statement quickly figured that Alex was the owner of the establishment and if it was cool with him who was he to question it?

"Now, tilt your head back a bit," Alex directed him, as he whisked the cream in the bowl a bit more.

Marco did as he was told, tilting his head back just enough so that his neck was clearly exposed for Alex to shave. Alex, taking the brush from the bowl now slathered Marco's stubble filled face and neck. Working the thick shaving cream across his skin Alex made sure that every inch was evenly coated. Once he was satisfied with his work, he placed the bowl on the counter and took up his straight edge razor.

"Ok, now, I know that there is some hot action going on behind us, but I need you to pay attention and stay perfectly still," Alex directed Marco.

"Yes Sir," Marco replied, as he shifted in his seat one last time.

Alex brought the razor to Marco's throat now. He skillfully worked the blade across his skin, holding Marco's head steady with his bare hand. The longer Alex worked, the more excited the man got, enjoying the intimate nature of the shave, not to mention the touch of his hands on his skin. He shut his eyes now, letting the barber complete his task without feeling as if he was studying his every move. The power Alex held over him was intoxicating. He loved the thought of how prone he was, and how trusting he had to be of the man as he ran the sharp instrument over his throat, chin and cheeks.

"Almost there," Alex noted, as he drew the last few strokes.

"Yes," Marco muttered.

"Just a few more strokes," Alex continued.

"Yes," Marco whispered, trying not to shift in the chair too much.

"Just, one, more, stroke," Alex noted.

"Yes!" Marco muttered a bit louder now.

"Perfect," Alex whispered, as he finished.

Marco took a deep breath and opened his eyes, focusing on his reflection. He almost didn't recognize himself. Freshly groomed and shaved clean, Marco had to admit that his partner was probably right when he told him that he looked far better cleaned up.

"There we go," Alex commented now, as he washed his equipment and proceeded to put it away. This gave Marco a few minutes to admire the man's work, as well as adjust himself before the drape came off.

Within minutes, Alex was back on him, applying the finishing touches. With a brush, a comb, more hair gel and a cool aftershave – which he nimbly applied to Marco's smooth skin – Alex brought the job to its climax.

"There. I think we are finished for today," Alex noted, as he tugged the cloth towel from around Marco's neck and whipped the silk drape off, exposing his suited form.

Marco sat there for a minute more until Alex finally addressed him.

"Oh, I'm sorry. Somehow I managed to get shaving cream on your pants," Alex commented now with an edge of surprise in his voice, as he looked down to see a rather large white stain that ran along the inside of Marco's dark pant leg.

"No!" Marco blurted out, with a wild look in his eyes, as he jumped from the chair. "I'll take care of that," he added, as he bolted for the restroom.

"Ok," Alex replied, with a surprised look on his face, as he watched his friend race off toward the back of the shop.

Marco dashed past Perry and Billy now, averting his eyes as he passed them.

Perry, with his eyes still tightly shut, was completely unaware of Marco's existence, and Billy, who was lost in his task, ignored the passing of the man as well.

Alex, while waiting for Marco to return, had the best view, as he watched from the front, eyeing the duo up as they continued to play unabashedly.

He watched, as Billy proceeded to suck and massage Perry's toes and foot. He watched, as Perry shifted in his seat with his right hand massaging the obvious bulge in his pants. Billy continued sucking, as Perry let slip a slight moan. Then, as Billy shifted and reached for the other foot, ready to remove that shoe as well, more than a moan was expelled from the seated man. Perry gasped aloud now, as he finished rubbing his groin and a broad smile slowly slid into place upon his face.

"Damn," Alex muttered to himself, as he continued to watch them, until Perry's eyes shot open.

Abruptly turning his attention away, Alex attempted to look busy, hoping that Marco would return soon from the restroom. Several minutes passed before he looked up again. As he did he caught sight of Perry and Billy quietly conversing. Then, he witnessed Perry leaning in and quickly kissing Billy's cheek. Averting his eyes once more Alex toyed with the polished buttons on Marco's suit jacket that he now had hanging over the chair behind the front desk.

"Ok, I think I'm ready to settle my bill," Alex heard Perry say, as he approached the counter.

"Sure. How did the shoe shine go?" Alex questioned the man.

"It was excellent. Your assistant has an amazing touch," Perry replied, as he slid into his leather jacket and glanced back toward the rear of the shop where Billy was still cleaning up his shoe shining supplies.

"Yes. He certainly knows his way around a quality shine," Alex noted, as he took the man's money and made the appropriate change from the register.

"Make sure he gets this," Perry instructed Alex, as he handed him not only a very generous tip, but also his business card.

"I will," Alex smiled. "See you in two weeks?" he added.

"Yes. You most definitely will," Perry replied with a broad smile of his own, as he turned now to exit the shop, giving Billy one more glance before finally leaving.

"Excellent," Alex replied, as he noted the appointment in the date book before him, briefly glancing up to watch the man exit.

Turning now, Alex faced Billy as he sheepishly approached the counter.

"I believe Mr. Richards was very pleased with your service," Alex commented, as he extended his arm with the tip and card in hand.

"I, uh, think he was," Billy beamed.

"But, next time, could you at least shine both shoes before you move on to...other business?" Alex commented, with a smirk on his lips.

"Yes Sir," Billy coyly replied.

"We don't want to get a bad reputation, by sending men out with half shined shoes. Do we?" Alex questioned his assistant.

"No Sir," Billy replied, just as Marco approached them.

"Reprimanding the boy?" Marco commented, as he took his suit jacket from the chair and slid into it.

"You could say that," Alex replied with a wicked grin, as Billy proceeded to fetch Marco's overcoat.

"Good," Marco replied. "You can't have that sort of thing going on around here. It could be bad for business. What sort of reputation do you want to get?"

"Yes. You're so right," Alex replied. "By the way, did that stain come out?"

"Uh, yes," Marco shyly replied now, as he slid into his overcoat, which the boy provided him with now.

"What stain would that be?" Billy chirped, as he stepped back to give Marco space now.

"None of your business," Alex replied. "Get back to work."

"Yes Sir," Billy replied, as he strode off, leaving the two men alone.

"Now, I will pencil you in for a cut in two weeks. It looks like I have an opening right behind Perry's appointment," Alex commented, as he stepped from around the counter, approaching Marco.

"Yes. That should work," Marco replied, as he fussed with his shirt and tie.

"Here. Allow me," Alex offered, as he reached up, with both hands, to straighten the crooked silk tie. "It's my fault it looks like this after all."

"Yes. Thank you," Marco replied now, allowing the man to set him straight.

"By the way, you should probably wear lighter colored pants next time," Alex whispered, as he leaned in. "It's easier to hide that way."

Marco pulled back now, locking eyes with Alex.

"Come now. Like I didn't know what was going on under that drape," he continued. "You must really think I'm nothing more than a dumb ex-model."

"I, uh, no...," Marco mumbled now, as he pulled away.

"Honestly. I'm flattered my friend," Alex replied with a huge smile on his lips.

"I should be going now," Marco suddenly replied, as he turned toward the door.

Alex let the man go, not wanting to fluster him any more than he already had. It wasn't until his friend was clearly through the door and outside on the sidewalk, that he suddenly took note of the sign swinging from it.

"Billy!" Alex called.

"Yes Sir?" Billy chirped, as he came dashing to the front. "Is everything ok?"

"The next time you turn this sign around to say CLOSED, consider yourself fired," Alex scolded the kid.

"Yes Sir," Billy replied, as he hung his blond head.

"Actually, let me rephrase that," Alex continued, with a very serious look on his face. "Consider yourself fired, if you don't at least give me a heads-up that you've gone and done that."

"Sir? I don't understand," Billy replied now, a bit worried and confused, virtually on the verge of tears.

"Come now. If I had known this, I would have taken more advantage of my customer as well," Alex replied, with a wicked smile on his face now.

"You're such an asshole," Billy chided his boss, punching him in the chest.

"Oh, really? Well this asshole is now all horned up and needs to find himself a way to release the build-up he is currently suffering."

"Well, the sign is still in the closed position," Billy playfully remarked, as he dashed off toward the back of the shop.

"That's right boy, which means you better run," Alex replied, as he fumbled with the buttons on vest, dashing off after him.

Torn

As Alex closed up his barbershop, his mind wandered a bit and ran through the somewhat erotic events of the day.

There was a moment, as he groomed his friend Marco, that he almost gave in to the situation and took the handsome man right there in the barber chair, but knowing that the guy had a partner waiting for him at home, slowed his advances. It wasn't until later, as he toyed with the notion of playing with his cute assistant Billy, that Alex realized just how horned up he had become over the situation.

"Damn," Alex muttered, as he slid into his warm, leather coat.

What's wrong with me, he questioned himself now, as he flicked the interior lights to the shop off.

Stepping outside, Alex locked up the shop, belted his three-quarter length coat and then reached for his leather gloves that he kept in his coat pockets.

"Hmm, that's odd," he noted aloud, as he found his pockets to be lacking his gloves.

Glancing through the front window, he looked to see if he had left them on the front counter or dropped them on the floor, but that didn't seem to be the case, as his eyes scanned the front of the shop, finding everything in order.

Oh well, he thought, as he turned and walked toward his car that was parked in the lot across the street.

Pausing, just outside the door to his car, he ran a hand inside his coat. As he searched the deep interior pocket, feeling for his car keys, he only turned up with a slip of paper with a name – Rafael Fabri – and a phone number on it. Digging, once more, into his exterior pockets, he continued to search for his car keys, but turned up empty handed. Beginning to panic, he soon searched all of his pockets.

"Damn. What the hell is going on?" Alex barked, as he leaned against the car, spinning the keys to his shop on his right index finger, wishing they were his car keys.

It then suddenly dawned on him...maybe this wasn't even his coat! Was that even possible?

Stripping it off, he gave it a once over under the nearby street light. It looked like his coat, but where in the world were his gloves and keys?

"Ok, Alex, calm down and think," he scolded himself, as he ran a hand through his thick head of hair.

Walking back across the street, he proceeded to unlock the shop and flick on the lights. Standing behind the counter now, his eyes played over its neat surface. Not a thing was out of place and there were no keys or gloves to be found anywhere.

"Fuck," Alex muttered, rethinking his day.

Sitting in the chair, behind the counter, he ran over the list of men who had been in during the day. Was it possible one of them had taken his keys or even possible that they took his coat and the contents?

Glancing over the names of the men, his mind whirled with the thought of having to call the dozen or more customers on the list. It had been a busy day and it was getting late now. He thought of calling Billy, who had gone home an hour ago, but he was certain his assistant would be of no help.

Then his thoughts went to the slip of paper that he had found in the coat pocket.

"Rafael," Alex muttered, as he traced the list of names from the day, once more, looking to see if any of them matched.

Soon, he found himself turning on his shop computer to cross-reference the entire database of his clients. Within minutes, there was a result of zero matches for a Rafael Fabri.

"Damn," Alex muttered. "Now what?"

As he turned the slip of paper over in his hand, he suddenly had the urge to call the number listed on it.

It's not all that late, Alex convinced himself. *Maybe this guy can tell me who has my coat and keys.*

Picking up the phone, he quickly dialed the number. Waiting for Rafael to answer, he toyed with the leather jacket before him, tugging on the thick belt that was used to tie it closed. It certainly looked like his coat, although, he had to be admit, this one looked a lot newer. It even had that fresh leather scent new coats tend to have.

"Come on. Pick up," Alex muttered to himself, as he grabbed a pair of scissors now, reflexively cutting the air with them.

SNIP. SNIP. SNIP.

"Damn," Alex moaned, as the man's automated voicemail clicked on.

Waiting for the beep, he decided to leave a brief message with the fleeting hope that the man would call him right back. He continued to wait, patiently, giving the man a few minutes to respond. As he sat there, his mind worked through the day once more.

Suddenly, it came to him.

"Perry," he muttered, as he remembered the man having a similar coat.

Actually, he suddenly recalled a conversation he had had with the man, several weeks back, over the coat, and how he was going to have to make a purchase of one.

Turning to the computer, he keyed in his friends name to retrieve his phone number. Picking up the phone, he called Perry, ignoring the note that Billy placed in the system that said not to bother this customer after 9:00 pm.

"Come on Perry, my friend, pick up, this is an emergency man," Alex muttered, as he returned to snipping away at the air with the scissors, in his hand, once again.

Again, there was no answer, just the sound of a voicemail clicking on.

Damn it. Doesn't anyone answer their phone these days? Alex thought, as he left a message at the beep.

Sitting there, discouraged now, he pondered what he should do about getting home. Calling a cab seemed to be his only option at 10:15 at night. Glancing out the front window, he noticed that it had started to rain as well. Walking home was no longer an option. It was definitely time to call a cab.

Reaching for the phone, Alex was startled a bit when it rang under his fingers.

"Hello," he said, as he picked up the receiver.

"Uh, yes, is this Alex Drake?" a smooth, deep voice questioned on the other end.

"Yes. The one and only," Alex replied.

"Good. This is Rafael. I just received your message," the man replied now.

"I'm sure you are wondering, Mr. Fabri, how I came upon your number, but I can assure you, it was an accident...," Alex noted now, as he fussed with his tie a bit, as well as the buttons on his vest.

"Oh, I'm not worried about how you came across me," Rafael replied with a soft chuckle at the end.

Alex began to explain his situation, until, rather abruptly, Rafael jumped in.

"Would you like me to come over and give you a ride?" the stranger offered.

"Uh, that's a bit generous, coming from a perfectly good stranger," Alex replied.

"Well, if you are a friend of Perry's, as you say, I do not consider you a stranger in the least," Rafael noted.

"Well, uh, thank you, but...I really wouldn't want you to go to any trouble," Alex replied, wondering why he was suddenly becoming a babbling idiot while speaking to this man with the beautiful, smooth voice. If he looked half as good as he sounded, Alex was sure he would be thankful to meet him in person.

"It wouldn't be a problem at all. Your shop is 10 minutes away," Rafael replied and abruptly hung up.

"Hmm, I guess I'll see you in a few," Alex said to the empty receiver.

Grabbing the leather jacket, Alex slid into it once more and proceeded to close up his shop for the second time. Stepping outside, he waited on the sidewalk, under the shops front awning, safe from the rain. Within minutes, a sleek, red sports car rolled up to the curb. Alex approached and leaned in, as the tinted, passenger side window quietly slid down.

"Get in," Rafael instructed Alex.

Without responding, Alex did just that, because, before him, sitting behind the wheel of the purring car, was the most stunning man he had ever seen. Truth told, he had seen some very attractive men during his days as a model, however, even with only the light of the dashboard illuminating his face, he could immediately tell, the man was radiant!

Sliding in, he turned to offer a hand to the man, which he quickly found enveloped in the softest, yet most masculine hand he had ever touched.

"It's nice to meet you Alex," Rafael cooed, with a slight accent that the barber had not noticed on the phone.

"Likewise," Alex replied, attempting to sound as equally seductive, locking eyes with the gorgeous man.

"Where to, me amigo?" Rafael questioned, partially slipping into his native tongue.

Alex dictated directions to him, which the man seemed to absorb without any hesitation.

As they pulled away from the curb, Alex relaxed a bit and began to soak in the powerful scents that lingered inside the enclosed, intimate space. The mixture of the leather interior with Rafael's cologne was intoxicating. The dark, warm capsule, as well as the soft hum of the car around them only added to the already stimulating situation.

Alex glanced over now, to catch a glimpse of Rafael, because even the man's mere profile was alluring!

With a strong chin and jaw, deliciously full lips and seductive, dark eyes – which were framed in beautiful, thick lashes – the man was truly breathtaking. Continuing along the man's body, Alex took in the details of the man's attire, as best he could in the dim lighting. Wearing a dark, long overcoat, Rafael appeared to have on a business suit under the coat. At his throat, the man wore a beautiful silk tie the color of a ruby...or so it seemed in the dim lighting. Alex imagined it matched the man's car, which, for some reason, only seemed natural.

"You're working rather late." Rafael suddenly commented to Alex.

"Yes. My shop closes around 7:00 on Sundays, but I had to finish up some end of the month paperwork," Alex replied now, as he attempted to lock eyes with the man once more, but failed, as Rafael remained focused on the rain slick road.

"I see," the man simply replied. "So, you found yourself abandoned and all alone, so you decided to call me."

"I, uh...," Alex began.

"It's perfectly alright," Rafael interrupted Alex, with a slight smile on his thick lips.

"Well, I sure appreciate this," Alex replied.

"Again, if you are a friend of Perry's, you are considered a friend of mine," Rafael added, with an even brighter smile, which exposed his perfect white teeth.

As they neared Alex's apartment, the barber suddenly felt the urge to invite the man up for a drink, or something, since he was so kind to drive him home.

"Nice," Rafael noted, as they parked at the curb and he eyed up the imposing warehouse-style building before them.

"It's in the middle of a remodel," Alex commented. "I just moved into the loft at the top. The other apartments are relatively empty at this point."

"I see," Rafael replied. "I would imagine the view from your loft is a beautiful one."

"Well, come on up and see for yourself," Alex suddenly extended the invitation before he lost his nerve.

"That sounds perfect," Rafael replied, as he put the car into park and turned the engine off.

The two men slid out of their respective seats, slammed the doors shut and dashed across the sidewalk toward the alcove that held the entrance to the complex. Even though the two acted quickly, they still managed to be doused with a fair amount of the driving rain. Safe under the front awning now, Alex turned, inserted his key – which, thankfully, he had on the same ring as his shop keys – and pushed the massive front door open.

"After you," he instructed Rafael, with an extended arm.

"Such a gentleman," Rafael replied, as he strode past Alex and into the hall beyond.

Alex was quick to close the door behind him and directed Rafael toward the end of the hall where a slightly tarnished, bronze, antique elevator stood. The elegant clock, positioned above the entrance, read 11:00 on the dot.

"This is all very nice," Rafael commented. "It reminds me of when I was in Europe."

"That does seem to be the style the designers were aiming for," Alex replied, as he called the elevator to their floor.

As the two men stood, waiting, Alex had the perfect opportunity to view his current companion better.

He took note of the man's stature now, which was several inches shorter than his own 6'3", but, from the way the man carried himself, he appeared much grander and powerful. He was indeed wearing a very handsome, dark, pinstripe suit below his expensive looking overcoat, which fit him perfectly. His rain sprayed hair was dark, thick and neatly trimmed, with every hair in its place. The clean-shaven, tan skin of his flawless face glowed, as droplets of rain trickled down the smooth surface.

"Ah, it comes," Rafael noted, as the doors to the elevator split open.

"Indeed," Alex replied, as he followed the man in.

The two men stood, only inches apart, as the dimly lit lift took them to the uppermost level of the building. As they neared the top floor, lightning, as well as thunder, began to shatter the dark, pitter-patter of the rain-filled evening. This could be seen through the skylight, located just above the elevator shaft, whereas the resounding thunder could be easily heard over the whirl of the elevator.

The ride was quick and they soon found themselves standing in the foyer to Alex's apartment.

"You will have to excuse the state of my place, but, as I said earlier, I just moved in," Alex informed Rafael, before turning the key in the heavy metal door that led to the loft.

"I'm sure it is far better than you think," Rafael replied, as he slid out of his overcoat, shook the rain from it, and folded it over his suited arm.

Sliding the door open, Alex motioned with his arm, as he did in the lobby, for Rafael to enter. He flicked the overhead lights on as he brought up the rear. Rafael, taking several steps into the apartment, paused now to drink in the spectacular view before him. Above, as well as to the left and right of him, were huge panels of glass, which afforded him a stunning view of the rain slick city streets below, as well as the violent sky above. He could also see all the way out to the harbor. As lightning danced through the rolling clouds, thunder rumbled below, sending obvious chills through Rafael's body.

"A drink?" Alex questioned the man.

"Yes, water would be perfect," Rafael whispered, as he continued to watch the storm roll by.

Within a minute, Alex was at his side, presenting him with his drink of choice.

"Thank you," Rafael replied in a hushed tone, as he subconsciously ran a hand over his silk tie to smooth it.

"Is everything ok?" Alex questioned the man, as he stood transfixed by the rain.

"Yes, I am sorry," Rafael replied, as he locked his dark eyes on Alex.

"No need," Alex replied, as he slid his leather coat off and offered to take Rafael's overcoat as well.

"Thank you," the man muttered, as he slowly stepped toward the closest window.

"So, if I may ask, where were you so late on a Sunday night, that you needed to be suited so sharply?" Alex questioned the man now, as he stepped up behind him.

"Why, I was waiting for a call such as the one I received from you," Rafael replied before sipping his water.

"Uh, I don't understand," Alex confessed, a bit confused.

"Let's just say, I had a hunch I would be heading out for a bit of fun tonight and leave it at that," Rafael replied.

"Ok. I suppose we could do that," Alex shrugged, as he took a sip of his own drink.

"So, may I ask you a question now?" Rafael questioned, as he turned to face Alex.

"Sure," Alex replied, matching the man's bold gaze.

"What are you doing with all of this rope?" Rafael inquired, as he extended an arm, bringing Alex's attention to the lengths lying around the apartment.

"Oh, that? The movers needed it to secure a few of the crates I had brought in," Alex replied, as he tapped a bundle of it that rested close to his wingtips.

"I see," Rafael replied, as he finished his drink.

"Why, were you thinking I was some sort of bondage nut?" Alex replied, with a chuckle.

"Well, one can always hope and dream," Rafael replied, with a dead serious look on his handsome face.

"Yes. I guess it never hurts to have an active imagination," Alex replied, as he stepped closer to Rafael with his fingers – unseen by the man – making a cutting motion near his thigh.

"No, not at all," Rafael confirmed, turning toward Alex.

"Such as, right now, I have this image in my head...," Alex started, as he moved even closer to the man, still silently snipping away at the air with his fingers.

"Yes?" Rafael questioned him with an inquisitive look on his face.

"The image is of a man. A very handsome man," Alex continued.

"Go on," Rafael prompted him, as their eyes locked. He could feel the man's warm breath on his skin now.

"He is beautifully suited, just as you are," Alex informed Rafael, as he stood mere inches away from him, gesturing to his suit, as the tips of his fingers brushed the sleeve of his jacket ever so lightly.

"I see," Rafael noted, as he ran a hand over his red, silk tie, suddenly feeling self-conscious.

"His suit is neatly tailored and rather expensive, as yours probably is," Alex continued, "but, and this is where things get rather wild Rafael, I have this urge to use my sharp scissors on him and his suit."

At this point Rafael fell quiet, eyeing Alex up and down, suddenly drawn to the cutting motion he was making with his fingers.

"I have this overwhelming urge to slice this man's suit to ribbons with my scissors," Alex admitted to Rafael without an ounce of guilt.

"Well, I guess that is only natural since you work with your hands," Rafael noted, as he took a casual step back now.

"Yes, I suppose that has something to do with it," Alex replied, as he turned away and dedicated his attention to the storm outside.

"Alex?" Rafael questioned.

"Yes?" he replied, as he watched the rain slide along the panels of glass above.

"You would never hurt someone while doing that...would you?" the man gently questioned.

"No, oh no, please, there's no need to worry. It's just a fantasy," Alex reassured the visibly shaken man, as he fought to make eye contact with him once more.

"Very well," Rafael whispered.

"Jeez, you must think I am some sort of madman," Alex noted now.

"No. Not at all," Rafael replied. "As I said, one can always hope and dream, but we should be careful about the things we actually do."

"Or the intense urges we actually act on," Alex suddenly found himself muttering aloud, as he eyed the length of rope at his feet.

"Excuse me?" Rafael replied, somewhat alarmed by the last comment.

"Nothing," Alex commented now with his eyes still focused on the rope.

"Well, maybe I should be heading home," Rafael suddenly replied, deciding it was a bad idea to stay much longer.

"No," Alex muttered, looking up now with a slightly wild look in his eyes.

"I think I really shou...," Rafael began to politely reply, but was abruptly interrupted, as Alex swiftly approached him and proceeded to devour his lips with his own moist and hungry mouth.

Rafael suddenly found himself trapped, held in Alex's strong arms, unable to break free. He let slip a deep moan within his throat, as the man continued to work on his mouth. He let slip the drinking glass in his hand, which soared to the hardwood floor and shattered into a million pieces.

This simple act only seemed to intensify the situation, as Rafael soon found himself being roughly manhandled, as if he were a simple child's toy. He soon became very aware of Alex's superior physical strength, as he found himself quickly – and easily – turned around and shoved against the closest wall.

"What the fu...," Rafael attempted to exclaim, but, once again, was unable to finish his sentence, having the wind knocked from him as he struck the hard wall.

"You are going to do as I tell you," Alex commanded now.

"Or...?" Rafael muttered, unable to see his assailant now, as he faced the red bricks before him.

"Or this can, and will, get very ugly," Alex whispered, as, ironically, yet befittingly, the sky lit up with several strikes of lightening, backlighting him perfectly, as if he were auditioning for the role of the psychopath in a horror movie. All that was missing was the maniacal laugh.

Rafael began to shudder, wondering what he had gotten himself into for the night.

"Now, let's start by reining in this volatile situation," Alex spoke, as he began to gather pieces of the rope from the floor.

Rafael attempted to glance over his shoulder, but failed, as Alex barked at him not to move.

"Listen, Raf, if you play along, you won't get hurt. It's that simple. It always is," Alex instructed the man. "If more people would just play along, the world would be a much better place."

Rafael remained in place, waiting, yet wanting nothing more than to make a break for the door, but it was far from where he stood and he knew he would never make it there in one piece.

"Ok. This may be uncomfortable at first, but I believe you are strong enough to withstand the pain," Alex informed Rafael, as he ran loops of coarse rope around the man's biceps, tugging each loop tighter as he worked his way up.

"Please, there is no need...," Rafael softly muttered.

"No need? I tend to disagree," Alex replied, as he finished the task of binding Rafael's arms. He turned him around now to look him in the eyes.

"Alex, please...," Rafael begged, as he shifted a bit in his bindings.

"Come on. Do you honestly think I'm going to hurt someone as beautiful as you? Just relax. We're going to have a little fun," Alex replied, as he walked away leaving the man standing there roped and ready to play with.

Rafael watched as Alex disappeared into a dark doorway, returning quickly with something in his hand.

"Remember that fantasy I just told you about?" Alex questioned Rafael.

"Yes," Rafael whispered.

"Well, I think it may be time to make it a reality," Alex replied, as he brought a pair of newly shined, silver scissors into view.

Rafael took a deep breath and focused only on the scissors now.

Alex, with a wicked grin on his face, slowly and silently started to cut the air with them.

"Do you mean to...?" Rafael started.

"I do. I hope this suit wasn't one of your favorites," Alex replied, eyeing it up and down.

Rafael didn't reply, knowing that he had very little choice now in the matter. If this man was going to cut his suit to ribbons, so be it, as long as that was all he was going to do.

"Now, Raf, don't look so concerned. I've heard Perry talk about his conquests and what he has done to them. If you know him, as I think you do, this situation shouldn't be anything new to you," Alex noted now, as he undid his own tie a bit more.

"Well, to be honest, Perry and I have never...," Rafael began, but, once again, found himself locking lips with Alex, although this time there was far less force and much more finesse.

Their mouths played back and forth, tongues working against one another, the juices of their moist mouths mixing. At times, the kiss was even soft, almost gentle, with their lips and tongues exploring, eager for more.

Alex was the first to pull back, staggering a bit as he caught his breath. Looking at the man before him, he suddenly felt a pang of guilt. What was he thinking? Did he really think he could just rope a man up and snip his beautiful suit to pieces? He had always dreamed of this moment, but now that he had the opportunity right in front of him, he wasn't sure he could go through with it.

He was torn.

His body was screaming for him to continue, but his mind was quickly working through the outcome, attempting to figure out if the price of performing this act was worth it. What would Perry think?

As the rain continued to pour and the lightening illuminated the dim scene Alex made the swift decision to proceed with his plan. He would deal with the consequences later. This man was gorgeous, suited, roped up and ready to play.

"Rafael. That's a beautiful name. Portuguese, is it not?" Alex questioned the man as he slowly approached.

"Yes," Rafael replied, keeping an eye on the scissors.

"With your subtle accent, I would assume that you have not always lived here," Alex continued, drawing in closer to his prey.

"No," Rafael whispered.

"Well, Raf, I think you will like it here. Even if it means exploring your surroundings, one inch at a time," Alex noted, as he proceeded to grasp the man's tie in one hand, while snipping away at it with his other.

SNIP.

The sound of the scissors cutting through the smooth silk was music to Alex's ears. It was subtle – yet piercing, in its own way, to Alex – as the metal of the scissor sliced across the fabric, freeing an inch of the man's tie from the pointed tip.

Alex let the snipped fabric fall gracefully to the floor, studying it as it sailed away, mesmerized by the sight.

Rafael watched now as his handsome, bright red, silk tie was snipped away, inch by inch. The tie had been one of his favorites, but he wasn't about to give this man the pleasure of knowing that.

Alex continued now, methodically working his way up toward the perfectly knotted top.

SNIP. SNIP. SNIP.

Three more inches taken away...

SNIP. SNIP. SNIP.

Nearly finished with the tie, Alex paused to look at his work.

"Excellent," he whispered, as he stood back, glancing from the severely cropped tie to the pieces on the floor.

"Does this excite you?" Rafael questioned the man.

"Very much so," Alex replied, as he rubbed the handle of the scissors across his bulging crotch.

"Continue," Rafael surprisingly prompted the barber.

"Oh, do not worry. We have a long way to go my friend," Alex replied, stepping closer now with his scissors at the ready.

Which would be next...Rafael's crisp white dress shirt or his beautifully tailored jacket? To Alex, they were both equally begging to slip under his sharp blade.

Once again, he was torn.

Alex's eyes were suddenly drawn more to the pure, stark white of Rafael's smooth, beautifully fitted dress shirt. He felt the overwhelming urge to slice into the flawless fabric. The untouched, crisp material was just crying out to be cut apart.

SNIP. SNIP. SNIP.

His nimble fingers worked the scissors through the air, slowly approaching Rafael.

"Do not move," Alex whispered, as he gently plucked the fabric away from Rafael's body and proceeded to work the tip of the very sharp scissors into it.

Rafael, unable to control himself, did flinch a bit as the blade pierced the cloth, but once it slid through and didn't slice deeper into his body; he was able to breathe again.

Alex worked the scissors vertically through the fabric, from just above the breast pocket to mid-chest, gently snipping away at the once unblemished cloth. As he did so, his eyes focused in on the tight, tan skin now revealed through the slit.

"Beautiful," he muttered, as he continued to work his instrument down, through the pocket.

Soon, he had an ample enough slit that he could work his fingers into the opening. Once he was able to do that, he found himself unable to control his urge to see more, and so he reached for the sides of the sliced fabric and ripped the shirt open even further.

The sound of the cloth ripping flowed over Alex's ears like waves rolling along a beach. He quickly realized that the noise made his cock jump inside of his own tailored pants. Actually, it made it throb, harden and ooze pre-cum, that's how powerful it was.

"Damn," he muttered, as his eyes traced along the line of exposed flesh that hc was viewing through the torn shirt.

Rafael's body was pure perfection.

The man's skin was flawless, pulled smooth and tight across bulging and perfectly toned muscles. His exposed pec was ample enough – with its brown, erect nipple – yet far from overdone in the way that many bodybuilders tended to do.

Alex wanted to clamp down on the exposed nip, but thought twice about it, figuring he would get lost in the motion and miss the opportunity to slice away the rest of the suit.

Moving to the right side of the man's body, Alex firmly took the pinstripe jacket into his hand and began to cut across the body of the coat. Again, once he had an ample slice worked through the fabric, he took the split sides in both hands and ripped it wider, tugging a bit so that the maroon-colored, satin lining gave at the same time the outer layer did.

That sound! Oh, fuck, that beautiful sound, his mind cried out, as his cock tented in his pants.

Taking his scissors in hand once more, Alex proceeded to snip away at the cotton dress shirt, cutting horizontally, so that the shirt just gave way to expose Rafael's beautifully crafted body.

SNIP. SNIP. SNIP.

Within seconds he had the man's gorgeous pecs and chiseled abs exposed.

"Fuck," Alex muttered, taking in the site of the man's body. "You're beautiful."

Rafael didn't reply, but oddly enough, was inwardly thankful that Alex appreciated his body, regardless of the fact that he was destroying his clothing.

Alex continued to work on the stark white shirt until he had it tattered and trimmed back in a way that framed the man's upper torso. With his arms bound back, Rafael was forced to thrust his pecs forward, giving Alex perfect access to his body.

SNIP. SNIP. SNIP.

His hands worked repeatedly, cutting away at the shirt and jacket, which sent chills to the very base of his erect cock, as the sound of the fabric ripping filled the air.

Taking a step back, Alex eyed his work.

Rafael truly was an Adonis and, to Alex, even more so in his sliced up suit.

Alex now approached Rafael and proceeded to lock lips with him once more, kissing him with great passion, as he ran his fingers over the curves and ridges of his exposed body. The erection in his own tailored pants was so obvious now that he couldn't help but not rub it against Rafael's suited leg.

"Alex, are you enjoying this?" Rafael muttered between kisses.

"Yes," Alex moaned.

The two kissed for several minutes more, letting the sound of the thunder and the rain play upon their ears, which mixed with the occasional moan or sigh expelled by each man.

Then, suddenly, Alex decided it was time to finish the job at hand.

Pulling back, he knelt, and began to work on Rafael's perfectly tailored pants. Snipping away the left pant leg, he quickly exposed the massive, muscular thigh held within, as well as a sheer, over-the-calf, sock, and a patent leather dress shoe. Next, he went back to work on his shirt, snipping away at it even more to further reveal Rafael's beautiful upper body. Soon, Alex found himself wanting to see more, which led him to the man's bicep that was bulging in the rope restraints.

SNIP. SNIP. SNIP.

Like music to his ears, Alex worked the scissors into the shoulder of the sleeve, cutting it away until he could work his fingers into the hole.

RIP!

Alex tore at the shoulder of the suit jacket, as well as the layer of shirt within, until he could see Rafael's smooth, tan skin.

RIP!

Moving to the opposite side, he did the same thing, but quickly found himself unable to stop at just that. Soon, he had the entire sleeve worked off both the suit and shirt, revealing the man's colossal bicep and forearm.

Alex took note of the tribal tattoo inked upon the man's upper arm. Was he a bit of a wild one himself?

Content with the damage done to the man's once beautifully tailored suit, Alex stood back, once again, to enjoy the vision before him.

Rafael stood there – bound – flexing his muscled body within the ribbons of his suit. He had the appearance of a man who just worked his way through a savage jungle, fighting to escape with his life and the torn remnants of his suit.

Alex turned and walked toward the wall now, flicking a switch located there.

Within seconds, sounds of a motor whirling filled the air, as a mechanism worked to open the skylight above Rafael. Shortly after that, the bound man, in his shredded suit, found himself doused with the cool rain of the ongoing storm.

Alex stood there and watched intently as the man tilted his head back to drink in the liquid as it rained down upon his face and body. He watched as Rafael twisted in his bindings, letting the water soak into the torn pieces of his suit. He watched as the man's perfectly cut muscles sparkled in the dim light, slick with streams of rainwater.

Taking one last moment to enjoy the sight, Alex slowly approached now, wanting nothing more than to take this man before him and ravage his gorgeous body.

The scissors, still gripped in his hand, shot out, striking Rafael.

SLICE.

The blade played through the saturated night air, striking the beautiful man.

SLICE.

The tip of the scissors cut deep, splaying open the surface it slashed.

SLICE.

Rafael moaned, unable to control himself, as the barber worked his instrument with great skill.

SLICE.

The man cried out, as he felt the cold metal play across his body.

SLICE.

The scissors soared through the air, nothing more than a silver blur.

SLICE.

Within seconds, Rafael found himself staggering back, gasping for air, as chunks of sliced rope fell to the floor, splashing in the puddle that was quickly forming there.

Alex stood, gasping, with scissors in hand, drenched from head to toe as his own tailored clothes clung to his body. He watched as Rafael groped for the nearest wall, his arms weak from being bound so tight.

The sound of the rain, splashing upon the hard wood floor, rang in their ears, as the thunder of the storm lessened and echoed only in the distance. Alex watched, as Rafael brought his dark gaze up. A look of confusion was set upon his handsome face.

Slowly, and without any coaxing, the tattered remains of his soaked suit began to slide off his slick body. One by one, the sliced pieces fell to the floor, causing Rafael, within seconds, to be completely naked – the only exception being his silk socks and leather shoes.

"Gorgeous," Alex exclaimed, as he stepped closer, examining his handy work.

Not a mark could be seen upon the man's flawless body. Alex had managed to slice the garments clear from his form without causing a single scratch, nick or cut. Rafael braced himself against the wall, unable to comprehend what had just happened. He certainly expected to be cut to ribbons himself, but that was not the case.

"Amazing," Alex noted now, as he stood before Rafael. "You remained flawlessly still so that I was able to complete my work."

Rafael leaned into the wall now, as he suddenly felt lightheaded. The situation overwhelmed him and he began to feel weak.

"Here, allow me," Alex spoke, as he stepped closer, offering him support.

"Yes. Please...," Rafael muttered, as he collapsed against him.

"You have been a most agreeable guest," Alex whispered, as he escorted the man toward a massive, brown leather couch situated in the living room.

"Well, you realize," Rafael began to mutter, "I may not charge you for the evening, but I am certainly sending you the bill for the suit."

"Excuse me?" Alex replied, slightly confused by this statement.

"Well, come now. How do you think I know Perry?" Rafael shot back, as he collapsed onto the couch and tossed his head back over the arm. "Do you think the two of us are just friends?"

"I just figured...," Alex started, but stopped mid-sentence.

"As I said, I won't charge you for the evening, since you didn't really 'get off,' but the suit will need to be replaced," he replied with a grin.

"Very well," Alex agreed, "but who says I didn't get off on this?"

Rafael looked up now and found himself staring at Alex's crotch.

The zipper, to his dress pants, was torn open, granting a spectacular view of his throbbing, cum soaked cock.

"I did that to you?" Rafael commented now, as he ran his tongue over his lips.

"Yes," Alex replied. "You did this to me. Well, drove me to do it to myself, but still..."

"Damn," Rafael replied. "I just may have to charge you for tonight."

"Oh really?" Alex replied with a mischievous look on his face.

Rafael smiled back, knowing that he wasn't going to do that, but the thought did cross his mind, as he realized the two of them were far from finished for the evening.

"Now, I could easily reconsider, if you allow me to work a little of my own magic," Rafael noted now, as he eyed Alex up and down.

"Ok," Alex played along, extending his arm with scissors in hand.

Rafael sat up now, and gently pushed the shining tool away. "I have no need for those," he stated with a grin, "I prefer to use my bare hands."

With that, Alex dashed off for the bedroom, with Rafael hot on his black and white, wing tipped heels. Somehow, a piece of rope managed its way into the naked man's hands just as he was leaving the living room. A wicked smile, upon his lips, was not far behind.

Riches to Rags

As Dante clawed his way up the rough hillside he struggled to make heads or tails of the ground below him. In the pale moonlight it was rather difficult to decipher much of anything, and with his slightly fatigued mind, it made doing that even worse.

He had been traveling for what seemed like weeks, but in reality it was only a matter of a few days. His mind and body were almost at their breaking point from lack of food and a good night's sleep.

"Fuck," he cursed, as he placed the palm of his massive hand down on a jagged rock. Thankfully, it didn't slice through his tough skin.

As he continued to clamor for the top of the hill filth and dust coated his torn jeans and sweat soaked tank top. He suddenly found himself gasping for air even though his extremely muscular body should have been able to take the climb in stride. He convinced himself that the difficult days of endless travel were the cause of this weakened state. He couldn't bear to think about the real reason why his entire body was so drained physically and, not to mention, mentally.

"Damn it. Just a bit further," he muttered as he pumped his huge, yet tired arms even harder, fighting to get to the top.

Finally, drawing his colossal, 6'4" frame up and over the edge of the slope he worked his thickly muscled legs so that he could stand erect on the ridge.

"No fuckin' way," he whispered in a raspy voice as he brushed back his greasy dark hair and took in the view before him.

There, basking in the light of the moon, as well as a run of low-lying ground sconces was what he quickly deemed an oasis.

The sanctuary, sitting in the valley below him was a sprawling estate which included a vineyard, stables, a tennis court and an in-ground pool. Dante was sure that he would find many other luxurious amenities within what appeared to be a gleaming diamond in the rough. After days of traversing the Italian countryside of San Marino this was a very welcome sight to his worn out body and mind.

Jackpot, he mentally exclaimed as he rubbed his filthy hands on his equally dirty jeans. His pale eyes scanned the beautifully kept compound for any signs of life. He knew he would do whatever it took to get inside the mansion, toward the center of the property, but he really wasn't in the mood to deal with another human being at this point in the game.

Fingering the crude metal lock pick he kept in the rear pocket of his jeans he cautiously moved down the gentle slop before him, silently approaching the grounds from the rear.

Before him, through the mixture of moonlight and shadows he could tell that he had clearly hit pay dirt stumbling upon this lavish, secluded manor. If the meticulous grounds surrounding the compound were a sign of things to come he was in for a rather enjoyable evening. It almost made the journey of the past few days more bearable knowing he would soon be kicking back as if he were a member of high society.

"Dante, you are one lucky bastard," he muttered to himself as he surveyed the grounds before him.

His skilled eyes flicked left and right, up and down, scanning for alarms, sensors or cameras set into the brick and steel wall surrounding the estate. To his surprise each security precaution was easily recognizable from where he stood. Either the people living here were too stupid to formulate a better system of protection or his skills had developed to a professional level, but either way he soon realized he had the advantage in the situation. Cracking this puzzle was going to take very little effort on his part.

Within minutes Dante found himself strolling around the inner grounds of the manor. As he slowly approached the main house he began to reason that the structure was currently devoid of life. A few well-placed exterior spotlights were the only source of illumination, as the house itself appeared somewhat dark.

Glancing down at his watch, with the cracked face, the current time of 9:02pm only helped support his theory. It was far too early for the residents to be in bed. Clearly, they were out for the evening or away for the weekend and – sadly enough for them – would return later to find their home ransacked from top to bottom.

"Well Dante, let's get this party started," he muttered to himself. "This is going to be a cake walk."

Circling the main house – a beautiful three-story brick structure with huge antique windows, a slate roof and many handcrafted details – Dante once again used his skills to detect any trace of a security system.

As before the devices were easily discovered and skillfully disarmed or avoided, allowing Dante the freedom to enter without causing alarm. The fact that the man moved with the grace of a panther hunting its prey allowed him to slip easily from shadow to shadow until he found the perfect access point.

Locating an oversized window toward the back of the house Dante slipped his massive frame through it with great ease. Regardless of the fact that he felt confident in his ability to disarm the security system he felt the need to play it safe and not utilize the door situated next to the window.

As he planted his heavy booted feet on the smooth stone floor and stood upright an unexpected coolness washed over him that instantly relieved his overheated body. He hadn't been aware of how humid the evening was until he found himself standing in the cool interior of the mansion.

Scanning the room Dante quickly realized he was standing in the homes very stylish kitchen. With a perfectly timed inward groan from his tortured stomach he knew this was the perfect place to start his 'tour' of the home.

Strutting across the room he soon found himself standing before the huge double doors of an upright refrigerator. Tugging the two sides open, Dante could instantly feel the uncontrollable drool forming on his thick lips. He was suffering from starvation and the delicious contents of this appliance would soon squelch that in seconds.

"Damn, whoever lives here eats like a fuckin' king," he noted to himself as he crammed handfuls of gourmet food into his mouth, foregoing the use of utensils, as well as any form of proper etiquette.

Finding that he was adequately stuffed he proceeded to wipe his food-coated hands down the front of his sweaty tank top. Walking away from the refrigerator now – which he left ajar – Dante continued along his path of discovery, eager to experience all of the pleasures this mansion held.

As he proceeded away from the kitchen and out into what appeared to be a main dinning hall he suddenly became hypersensitive to his filthy, smelly body, for around him he found a polished, pristine, flawlessly decorated room. Even the crisp, cool air, lightly scented by the fresh flowers found in the middle of the massive oak table before him reminded Dante of his disgusting state.

"I need a shower," he whispered to himself as he eyed up the double wooden doors on the opposite side of the room.

Approaching, he slowly slid them open with his grimy hands to reveal an amazing main foyer, which contained a massive staircase leading up to the second level.

"Perfect," Dante muttered, as he cautiously ascended the plush, carpeted steps before him.

Reaching the second floor landing he glanced out the wide window found there and took in the view of the yard below. He could easily make out the shimmering surface of the pool as well as the stone patio. He wondered if he would have time to enjoy a swim before the owners returned.

This place is too good to be true, he thought to himself as he continued up the stairs.

Arriving on the second level Dante had four choices before him – further up, straight ahead, left or right. Deciding that it was in his best interest to scout the entire house first he continued up to the third floor, figuring it was best to start at the top and work his way down.

Stepping onto the third level he found himself with only two options this time – left or right. Turning left he skulked down the hall toward the single door located at the end.

Opening the door he soon found himself in what appeared to be a private office and library. Thousands of books lined the walls and toward the rear of the room sat a massive wooden desk with a handsome, high-backed leather chair. Upon the desk sat a state-of-the-art computer system.

As Dante stepped into the room his attention flew toward a well-stocked liquor cabinet located just to the right of an immense, stone fireplace.

"Excellent," he whispered. "I could use a drink."

Reaching for the brass handle on the case, he attempted to tug it open only to find a bit of resistance in the form of a lock.

"Well, this won't do," he spoke aloud, as he quickly decided that he didn't have the patience to pick it.

Turning to face the fireplace Dante reached for the sharp, metal poker, took a hold of it in his massive paw and whirled around to make contact with the glass door of the case, shattering it into a thousand pieces.

Moving forward after dropping the heavy poker he reached into the broken case and undid the lock from within. For some reason he found great pleasure in destroying the front of the case, even though he could have easily picked it.

Removing several bottles from within the case Dante worked his way over to the handsome desk. Once behind it he collapsed into the leather chair, twisted the bottles open and proceeded to drink himself into a comfortable stupor. The sensation of the expensive liquids playing over his throat was extremely satisfying. Within minutes he found himself floating along on a serious buzz, which quickly led to a sloppy state of drunkenness.

"Well, Dante, you have yourself here a rather beautiful situation," he noted to himself, as he raised a bottle in his hand. "Cheers!"

Emptying the bottle he tossed it across the room. Even in his slightly intoxicated state he managed to get it into the fireplace, where it bounced around a few times before shattering.

Turning to the computer he groped for the mouse and was inwardly pleased when the flat screen monitor came to life. The system was on and active. He quickly decided to have some fun before moving on.

Within seconds, even with his hazy mental state, he had the security system for the mansion on screen. Once it was up and running he was able to scroll back through the logs to see if he had accidentally tripped a silent alarm along the way. From what he could tell he hadn't. He also took note of when the system was last set. It appeared to be only several hours before, around 6:00pm, by someone named Giovanni De Luca.

"Excellent," Dante purred as he relaxed a bit more, knowing the owners name, as well as the time he left. A quick glance at the man's desk calendar supplied Dante with the reason for the man's departure – *Daniel's 40th! Cocktails, 7:00pm sharp, with dinner to follow. Bring wine.*

Rolling out from behind the desk he stood and made his way toward the door. From what he just saw on the screen it appeared that the master bedroom and bath were on this floor.

Heading down the hallway he found himself standing before a set of ornate doors. Carved into the wood were the intertwined forms of nude, very muscular men.

"Interesting," Dante noted as he reached for the thick doorknob and twisted it.

Pushing the elaborately designed doors open he entered the bedroom – he assumed – belonging to Giovanni.

Immediately he focused on the four-post bed that sat in the center of the room. Even in the pale moonlight that was filtering through the dozen or more floor to ceiling windows Dante could tell that it wasn't a traditionally designed bed. Clearly, the same artisan who created the doors to this room did this piece of furniture as well, because, instead of four standard posts, there were four beautifully crafted nude males done in a dark wood, holding the heavy, silk canopy up.

As Dante slowly approached the bed he could make out the details of each man more clearly. He decided that whoever the artist was they had an amazing talent for erotic carvings. If he hadn't already scanned the security system for other signs of life – which there were none beyond his own – he could have easily mistaken these four statues for real men.

"Well, we seem to have ourselves here a lover of the arts as well as the male form," Dante muttered as he placed the liquor bottle he had been sipping from on the nightstand and began to slowly run both of his hands over one of the nude forms.

Lost in the details of the carving Dante soon found himself oddly aroused.

"Ok man, calm down," he spoke to his bulging crotch as if it had a mind of its own. "It's time for a nice, very long, scalding hot shower."

Turning away from the bed Dante strode across the wide expanse of the room, heading for, what he hoped to be, the master bathroom.

As he entered the dark hallway leading off of the bedroom he took note of the double doors to his left and right, but it was the opening straight ahead that drew his attention the most.

Before him, framed in heavy, silk drapes appeared to be the entrance to Giovanni's inner sanctuary. As he passed through the doorway, he stopped dead in his tracks as a faint glow began to illuminate the room. Quickly, he reasoned that there had to be a sensor somewhere that prompted this to happen as an individual entered.

Scanning the chamber his eyes played across the lavish ornate surroundings that now basked in a warm, albeit simulated, candlelight glow.

In the center of the room sat an enormous marble tub, which, because of its scale looked more like an indoor pool. Situated around it were more erotic carvings of nude males but these were done in marble to match the tub. Mixed in with the statues were dozens of exotic plants as well as many glass sconces which Dante imagined looked magical when fully lit. Floor to ceiling windows encircled the tub, creating the illusion of being outdoors. A stone backdrop, situated on the center wall only enhanced this illusion. Dante imagined that the structure created a waterfall effect, once activated, that poured into the immense tub below.

To Dante's right stood a glass-encased shower, large enough for six or more strapping men to enjoy at once. To his left ran a bank of sinks with several ornate mirrors set into the wall above.

Taking several steps to the left Dante soon found himself fascinated by his own reflection in the oversized mirror. He had not realized, until this moment, how unkempt and wild his current image was.

His thick, black, usually silky hair was matted and greasy, hanging in tendrils around the sharp angles of his rugged face. The five-o-clock shadow that ran along his strong jaw and encircled his full lips was on the verge of becoming a full fledged beard. His once smooth, pale skin was now a golden brown from spending hours in the sun and his bright blue eyes were bloodshot and heavily lidded from lack of sleep.

"Damn, Dante, you look like shit," he muttered to himself as he began to work the tight, filthy tank top from his upper body.

Sliding it up and over his substantial, slightly hairy pecs he proceeded to bunch it up into a ball and toss it to the tiled floor. Next, he kicked off his dirt-encrusted boots, which then afforded him the opportunity to strip off his jeans. Tugging on the button fly to his skin-tight denims, Dante, at first, found it somewhat difficult to work them off, as his bulging crotch continued to throb and grow. However, soon enough he was able to work them off, revealing two very thickly muscled thighs and equally massive calves.

He now stood, virtually naked in his worn, slightly soiled jockstrap and cotton socks. The material of his strap was so shabby that several holes could be seen along the front pouch, giving a sneak peek to what was held within. The socks, once a crisp white were now the color of grey dirty bathwater.

Turning toward the shower Dante reached in and rotated the brass dial until a constant stream of water was pouring from the main disk shaped showerhead.

"Hmm," he moaned, as he felt the cool water slowly turn warm upon the skin of his wide forearm. "That feels so good."

Stepping away from the shower he bent now and slowly rolled the socks from his feet, adding them to the growing pile of discarded gear. The last item to remove was his jockstrap, which he tugged at and let slide down along his ample legs until the elastic loops rested around his thick ankles. Stepping out of the strap he kicked it into the pile as well. He was glad to be free of the slightly uncomfortable jock. He briefly wondered how the rugby player he stole it from could stand wearing such a thing.

Standing completely naked now he turned to catch another glimpse of his body in the mirror.

In the dim light Dante appeared as flawless as the six marble statues that surrounded the tub next to him. Every inch of his body was carved to perfection. Every inch was pushed to its limit. Every inch, regardless of the pain and suffering of the last few days was striking beyond words.

"Ok man, I take back that 'you look like shit' comment I made earlier," he spoke to his own reflection. "You are one fuckin' fine-looking beast."

Flexing in the mirror Dante was once again mesmerized by his own image.

His muscles rippled and rolled, bunching and bouncing in all the right places as he continued to strike several poses. He continued to do this, until finally, his thick, throbbing cock slapped against his thigh, reminding him that it had grown to twice its size in the last 15 minutes.

"Ok, I'll take care of you soon enough," he muttered to the oozing serpent as he tugged on it a bit after running a hand over his massive scrotum sac.

Slipping into the extra-large glass shower Dante let the water drench his body, washing away the dirt and grime that coated him, as well as the tension of the past few days.

"Oh, fuck, this feels amazing," he moaned as his massive hands groped for one of the many varieties of soap and body lotions arranged along a glass shelf inside of the shower.

He continued to rub and caress his massive frame, stroking his thick tense muscles up and down. The sensation of the scalding hot water rolling over his worn body was somehow both relaxing and rejuvenating. He could feel it melting away the stress that had pent itself up in his back and neck.

His soap slick paws continued to work over his ample pecs until his brown nipples became fully erect. They then slid down over the ridges of his chiseled six-pack, until finally resting upon the throbbing muscle between his oversized legs.

Taking the smooth, fat hose into his hands he proceeded to roll back the foreskin until the plump, bulbous head of his cock was fully exposed. Rubbing it with both hands he found himself fully charged and erect within seconds. Barely cupping his fleshy balls with one huge hand he began slowly stroking his oozing prick.

"Oh Dante, yeah...," he moaned, as he worked it up and down, power stroking his meat.

Working his thick, flesh stick he could feel the load building in his balls, but he soon found himself letting the pre-cum slick prick drop from his hand. Dante suddenly had the urge to edge a bit before blowing his load. He knew when he finally did release that it would be a massive blast and he was looking forward to experiencing that.

Returning his focus to cleansing his body he began to lather up his dark, greasy hair with a scented, herbal shampoo. The creamy substance felt wonderful on his scalp, tingling and revitalizing his thick unruly mane. He began to wonder if he could become accustomed to such expensive bath products because lately he was lucky if he had a cheap bar of soap at his disposal. Luxuries such as these had somehow become foreign to his body.

Finishing in the shower Dante strode from the glass chamber, across the tiled floor, back toward the sinks.

He once again stood naked before the mirror inspecting his muscular form that was now slick and refreshingly clean. The remaining rivulets of water ran across his muscles, dipping in and out of the tight curves and deep crevices. His soaked pubes clung to the base of his erect cock as the drenched locks of his head plastered themselves along his thick neck, high forehead and sharply angled cheeks. Grabbing a towel he began to dry himself off, toying a bit with his throbbing tool, but not giving in to the desire to stroke and shoot.

Once sufficiently dry he proceeded to wrap the soft, cotton towel around his narrow hips. He found it somewhat amusing that the fabric tented like a circus big top in the front while clinging to the firm globes of his muscled ass in the back.

"Ok Dante how about a shave?" he spoke to his reflection. "I'm sure Giovanni has a few top of the line grooming tools around here somewhere."

Searching the cabinets located close to the sinks he soon had the necessary items to complete his transformation from disgusting dud to dapper dandy. Within minutes Dante was once again clean-shaven. His smooth, tan skin glowed as he applied an aftershave and moisturizer. It had been weeks since he looked or even felt this civilized.

"Now, for the hair," he mused as he continued with his self-inflicted makeover.

Spending several more minutes before the mirror Dante soon had every thick, silky hair in place.

"I think that's good for now," he finished fussing. "How about we find ourselves something to wear? Can't walk away from this place naked," he joked with his reflection.

Turning his broad back to the sinks he sauntered out of the room and back into the master bedroom. As he walked the towel around his hips began to loosen. Pausing in the hallway between the two rooms Dante soon found himself fully exposed once again, as the wrap dropped from his waist and pooled on the floor around his huge feet.

"Left or right?" Dante questioned as he eyed the sets of double doors he assumed led to Giovanni's closets.

Taking a step to the right, Dante grasped both bronze handles and yanked the doors open. As he did this a rich, warm light came to life inside the room before him – and it most certainly was a room, not a mere closet as he had once assumed.

Stretching out before him were rows and rows of clothing: on racks, in bins and on display mannequins. It was like stumbling upon a private men's department store.

"Damn, if I can't find something to wear here I'm in trouble," he muttered, but quickly realized that there was a good chance the owner of these garments wasn't as massive in stature – few men stood as tall or as built as Dante.

Entering the room, he approached the closest rack of clothing, which was a run of beautifully tailored suits. Pawing his way through the expensive articles he searched for the size label on each. It appeared, to his surprise that there was a wide assortment of gear in many different cuts and sizes.

"Now why would a man need so much clothing and in so many freakin' sizes too?" Dante muttered as he continued his half hazard hunt, letting $3000.00 suits – which were not his size – fall to the floor. "Then again, who am I to question the eccentric actions of the rich and famous?"

Soon, he had piles surrounding him as he tore through each section, leaving behind only the items he felt would suit him. Caught up in a drunken frenzy Dante found himself yanking and ripping items off their hangers. Neatly tailored suits and gorgeous, thick top coats, as well as freshly pressed shirts all went flying through the air in tatters.

Suits – with designer labels that read Valentino, Dolce & Gabbana, Gucci, Calvin Klein and Yves St. Laurent – were soon reduced in Dante's powerful hands to nothing more than mounds of ruined, frayed cloth. Top coats – in sizes too big or too small, done in wool, leather, cashmere, suede and even fur – found their way to the floor, destroyed in the process. Dress shirts – in warm and cool solid colors, as well as wide and narrow stripes, many with French cuffs and spread collars – were added to the mix.

"Fuck you, you rich bastard," Dante barked as he continued to ravage the room.

As he worked his way toward the back of the chamber, shredding most of the items in his path, he soon found himself confronted by a wall full of nothing but formal wear.

"Damn, who does this guy think he is, James Bond?" Dante spat as he stumbled toward the wall before him.

Reaching into the lineup of tuxedoes hanging before him he grabbed several with his large hands and tossed them to the floor. Standing over the pile of eveningwear, still completely naked, he began to stroke his still erect cock. Within seconds Dante found himself emptying his suddenly full bladder.

A hot, golden stream of piss struck the satin lapels and silk linings of each discarded suit. The liquid either slowly soaked in or quickly pooled upon the material, depending on the make or texture of the fabric. The torrent of foul fluid continued for many minutes more, until, in the end, each garment was officially saturated. In particular, Dante ensured that the all white tux, lying among the pile, was thoroughly soaked through. He stood and watched as the once smooth and flawlessly white material turned a sickening shade of yellow.

Grasping his cock he shook it roughly, letting the last few drops splatter and then mockingly belched, "Shaken, not stirred, Mr. Bond, just as you like it!"

With that, he continued on his course of destruction, eradicating every suit, tuxedo, overcoat, and shirt that did not fit him. He wasn't leaving a piece of wearable clothes behind, beyond what suited him. By the time Dante was finished he was left with roughly a dozen of each type of garment, forty-six pieces in all, which he would be taking with him, assuming Giovanni owned more than one car.

Strutting out of the room and across the hallway he tugged on the matching set of double doors, wondering to himself what would be found behind door number two. As a similar light came to life, illuminating the room before him Dante could quickly deduce that this room held the accessories to the garments of the first room.

Shoes and boots in every shape, size and color lined the entire left wall, with drawers of socks and garters found below the angled shelves. Ties with matching pocket squares hung halfway down the right wall, and undergarments for all seasons could be found in drawers beyond this colorful display, along with belts and suspenders. In a tall, wide, wooden cabinet set off by itself Dante discovered drawer after drawer of cufflinks and shirt studs, tie clips, necklaces, bracelets, earrings, rings and watches in an endless array of styles and colors.

"Hot damn, the mother load," he whispered as his eyes played over the virtual treasure trove set before him.

Drawing his attention away for a brief moment his eyes wandered to the end of the room where floor to ceiling mirrors were set along with several dressing tables filled to the brim with skin lotions, moisturizers, aftershaves, colognes, nail files, clippers and combs.

Returning his gaze to the watches in the case before him he quickly took note of the time - it was almost midnight. He had been in the house for just about three hours and still no sign of the local law enforcement or the inhabitants of the estate.

"Well, I guess it's time to freshen up, suit up and get the hell out of here," he muttered to himself as he glanced at his slightly damp, naked form. Because of his recent trashing escapade he found his body coated in a thin layer of perspiration. Heading back to the shower he quickly cleansed his massive form again.

Freshly showered he sauntered back to the room filled with accessories and rooted through the drawers of undergarments, selecting a fresh pair of cotton boxers as well as a skin-tight, cotton undershirt. The smooth, cool fabric of the shirt stretched to its very limit over his enormous pecs and the shorts expanded perfectly to hold his throbbing cock and seed-filled balls.

Turning, Dante advanced upon the wall of shoes and socks, quickly selecting a pair of each, in black. Sitting in a high-backed leather chair situated in the middle of the room he worked the silky smooth, over-the-calf-socks onto his feet. The golden tips formed perfectly around his toes and the tight band at the opening hugged his rock hard calves flawlessly.

Standing, with shoes in hand, he proceeded back to the first room and selected an outfit from the remaining pieces for his getaway.

This evening, drawn to the darker colored clothes, Dante decided on a rich, silky, plum-colored dress shirt. As he slid into it the soft material caressed the hairs of his forearms, sending a shiver to his very core. Leaving the cuffs, as well as the front buttons undone he reached for the pants of a black-on-black pinstriped suit. Sliding into these he soon felt a tingling sensation inside his cotton shorts as his throbbing cock responded to the feeling of the silk lined trousers stroking the skin of his massive thighs.

"Damn, now back to room number two," Dante muttered as he began to tire of not having everything he needed to suit up right before him in one place. He quickly convinced himself that the owner, Giovanni, had to have a manservant of some sort who probably selected everything his master needed for an evening out.

Approaching the cabinet of jewelry he selected a matching set of sapphire, black and silver cufflinks and shirt studs. Working them into the cuffs and front of the neatly tailored shirt Dante found it somewhat alarming that the garment fit him perfectly. It encased his substantial upper body beautifully with just enough room to breathe.

Next, he selected a black snakeskin belt with a chunky, silver buckle. Running it through the loops of the pants he soon realized that the item was more decorative than functional, for the pants hugged his frame – in particular, his rock hard, round bubble butt – as flawlessly as the shirt.

Finally came the moment to select yet another decoration – a tie and pocket square, of which there were many. Perusing the selection his eyes quickly went to a purple and silver striped set which seemed to match the links and studs he chose just a minute before.

"Damn, this guy has it all figured out," Dante chuckled as he worked the silk tie into a thick, full Windsor.

Sitting, once more in the leather chair he worked on the black leather dress shoes he had chosen earlier. Resting for a minute his eyes suddenly caught sight of a pair of ankle high leather dress boots. Kicking his current footwear off, which shot through the air, striking one of the full length mirrors at the end of the room, he reached for the boots and proceeded to work them onto his size thirteen feet as the struck mirror tumbled to the floor in sharp slivers.

"Once again, a perfect fit!" he barked, as he stood now, reaching for the suit jacket he had draped over the arm of the chair.

Heading to the jewelry cabinet once more he selected a watch, two rings and a tie clip.

Turning, Dante went to exit the room with the suit jacket folded over his wide arm, but, abruptly, he found himself confronted by a formally suited man who stood in the doorway, blocking the exit.

"I believe you forgot your pocket square," the man noted with a stern look on his handsome face.

"Fuck," Dante muttered, suddenly feeling as if he were a kid caught with his hand in the cookie jar, although, those kids usually didn't have a revolver pointed at them.

"Well, Mr. De Luca would you like to help me pick one out?" he boldly had the nerve to ask the armed man - who he safely assumed was the owner of the estate - as he slid into the suit jacket.

"Hmm, how about if we let the officers help you with that when they get here," the older man replied with a slight smirk on his lips.

"Oh, so, the game is over already? You don't want to have a little fun with me yourself?" Dante replied as he looked the man over, taking in his equally massive frame, which was beautifully suited in a double-breasted tuxedo.

"No. Regardless of how dashing you currently look in my suit I have no interest in messing around with a vagrant such as yourself," Giovanni replied.

"That's a shame, because I think the two of us would have one hell of a wild time," Dante replied as he took several long steps forward, quickly closing the gap between them.

Giovanni stood his ground and locked eyes with Dante. He didn't dare let the man get the upper hand in the situation.

Dante, drinking in the man's scent, matched his steady gaze as he slowly shifted deeper into his personal space.

"I hope you enjoyed your reckless romp through my home, because it's going to be awhile before you are able to do that again," Giovanni noted. "By the way, I hear the local prisons are rather rough on men like you."

"Oh yeah, and what makes you think I can't take it or give it back just as rough?" Dante retorted with an air of cockiness.

"I'm sure you can my friend, although once I finish re-suiting you up the guys in prison are not going to know what to make of you," Giovanni replied with a wicked grin on his handsome face.

"What is that supposed to mean?" Dante replied, suddenly feeling a bit less confident in his position.

"Oh, you'll see. Now move," Giovanni motioned with the tip of the gun for Dante to exit the dressing room.

Leading him out to the bedroom Giovanni switched on several lights and made Dante stand in the center of the room with his arms extended.

"Now, I'm going to call my manservant, Andre, and my driver, Bruno in here and they are going to help me undress you *and* redress you," the man coolly stated. "Then, we are going to let the authorities take you into custody. No questions asked."

Dante, suddenly worried where this was heading, thought of making a move for the door, but glanced at the gun and quickly rethought his actions.

"Actually, I think you'll be very happy where you are headed," Giovanni noted, as he moved toward the double doors. "Ok, boys, come on in and give Dante here a hand."

The man flinched as Giovanni used his given name, which had not been mentioned by him at any point since they met.

"Don't look so surprised boy. Your exploits of the last few days have been all over the news. It was pretty easy to put two and two together," Giovanni stated blankly, as Dante's attention was suddenly drawn toward the two guys entering the room.

It was as if the marble statues in the bathroom had come to life. Strutting into the room were two massive, muscular, uniform-attired brutes. Andre, the manservant, towered over Dante, while Bruno easily blocked out Giovanni with his broader, thicker form.

The two swiftly approached Dante and began undressing him – roughly!

Bruno, with his massive paws grabbed the two lapels of the suit and tugged on them until they gave, splitting away from the body of the jacket in one very long, very audible...

RRRIIIIIIP!

Andre was next with a far quicker strike, yanking on the breast pocket with one hard tug until it too gave, which took mere seconds.

RIP!

Next, each of them took a sleeve and, starting at the cuff, tore them up to the shoulder, until each one was on the verge of coming free.

RIP! RIP!

Buttons were broken off. The lining of the jacket was torn out along with the inner pockets. The vent in the back of the jacket was split all the way up to Dante's neck. The tailored, once beautifully crisp dress shirt – now soaked through with perspiration – was also worked over, its studs yanked off and sleeves treated the same as the suit jacket. The dress pants that once hugged Dante's ass perfectly barely covered him at all now.

RIP!

SNAP!

RIP!

Within minutes Dante was left staggering about in a ruined suit, one that barely hung from his muscular body in tatters and ribbons. The only two items left unmolested were the silk tie and the leather boots.

"So, Dante, how does it feel to go from rags to riches, back to rags once again?"

Dante, stunned, wasn't sure how to reply to the man, for he had never been handled the way he just was and he had a feeling this treatment would continue with his impending imprisonment.

"Now, since you seem to have turned into a man of few words let's proceed with your redressing," Giovanni noted, as he motioned for Andre and Bruno to completely strip Dante naked. "I think you'll really enjoy my choice of garments for your forthcoming confinement. As I noted earlier the guys in prison are going to have a field day with you!"

An absolute field day, Dante thought to himself as he eyed up the two men approaching him. *A day you'd pay dearly to witness...you rich bastard.*

T.J.

As Cal approached the stadium locker room he paused just outside the open doorway to make sure that the coast was clear before he entered. He knew he was about to go where he didn't belong and seeing as he was suited from head to toe in the finest set of formal wear available he also knew there was going to be little he could do if he needed to blend in at a moments notice.

Moving along the tiled hallway that led into the stuffy, malodorous chamber Cal wondered if he should slip out of his patent leather shoes which were clicking upon the floor rather loudly. Clearly his silk encased feet would draw less attention, but he soon realized that if he needed to make a quick get away he would probably need the slightly better traction of his imported shoes. Most likely in his socked feet he would slip and slide all over, falling on his ass in an instant.

Continuing along his path Cal cautiously made his way into the main locker room where the walls were lined with the open stalls used by the players. Each one had the players name posted above it so it was relatively easy to find the one he was looking for.

"Roberts. Trevor. Jameson...Thom Jameson." the tuxedo-clad man muttered as he reverently approached the third booth after placing his top hat on the wooden bench.

There, laid out before him, was exactly what he came looking for.

Jameson's stall was filled with his recently discarded baseball gear. Tucked neatly in the cubby above was his cap and helmet. Hanging loosely upon the hooks found within the long booth were his jersey and pants.

Tossed carelessly upon the floor was his undershirt, socks, and...

Cal's mind suddenly whirled at the sight of the last item that sat so innocently, so quietly among the pile of discarded gear. Tucked just below the saturated cotton t-shirt and resting squarely atop the rolled up soiled socks was Jameson's jockstrap.

"Hmm, the treasure I've been searching for," Cal whispered, as he extended a slightly shaky hand toward the item of his desire.

The second his fingers touched the broad elastic waistband he felt a jolt of excitement fly through his body, causing his heart to race even faster. Attempting to remain calm Cal worked to steady his hand as he drew the strap out of the damp pile. Inspecting it with lustful eyes he slowly brought the mesh pouch, which recently held Jameson's manhood, closer to his face. Inhaling deeply, the formally attired man drank in the raw, pungent odor found within. Intoxicated by the aroma he began to swoon a bit in his dress shoes. Inebriated, Cal found himself swiftly erect and throbbing within his neatly tailored slacks.

He continued, with his eyes closed, to sniff the moist fabric, until someone exclaiming, "What the fuck?" abruptly snapped him out of his euphoric state.

Dropping the jock Cal's dark eyes flashed open to take in the sight of the person who was now advancing on him. In the blink of an eye he swiftly found himself pinned up against the tiled wall with Jameson's handsome face mere inches from his own. However, the player's face was contorted into a look of outrage, which lessened his overall attractiveness – to a degree.

"I'm sorry! I didn't mean to...," Cal began to sputter as he struggled to free himself.

"I'm sure you didn't!" Thom spat back as he tightened his grip. "You shouldn't even be down here."

"I know. I know. I'm sorry," was all Cal was able to muster, as he began to become all too aware of the player's body pressed against his own – the player's naked, slightly damp body.

"You should be upstairs pretty boy, that's where the stadium is holding their stupid charity event," Thom growled. "Not down here sniffing around. You could be severely punished for doing what you're doing."

Mustering a bit of dignity Cal boldly replied, "My brother is an officer. I know my rights. It's not a crime."

"The hell it isn't!" Thom barked. "What's your name, bitch?"

Cal remained silent, locking eyes with the powerful blonde as the player's naked form pressed firmly against the exquisite and expensive fabric of his tuxedo. He could feel sections of his pants going moist from the exposure to Thom's wet flesh.

"I asked you a question, buddy. I think it would be in your best interest to answer me!"

"Cal Michaels."

"I see. Well, Mr. Michaels, perhaps I should take matters into my own hands. Perhaps, since you seem to be really into me, sniffing my damned jockstrap and all...I should return the favor and get into you. If you know what I mean...," Thom daringly informed him with a wicked smile upon his lips.

"Let me go," Cal demanded as he began to thrash a bit, feeling the player's throbbing rod along the side of his leg. "Let me go, now!"

The wicked smile quickly melted away as the player slowly softened his grip right along with the expression on his tan face.

"Fine. You know what...go! Get the fuck out of here you piece of shit," Thom suddenly spat as he pulled himself off and turned away.

It was in this instant that Cal gained the upper hand. Launching himself at the player he swiftly managed to tackle him to the ground. Landing hard upon the jock's tight body he could hear the wind released from his lungs. Thrashing and moaning the two men wrestled, until Cal was able to successfully pin Thom to the floor.

"I'm not going to hurt you!" Cal yelled. "So, stop fighting me!"

"You fuckin' asshole!" Thom howled.

"I said...I'm not going to hurt you!" Cal continued as he fought to calm the bucking stud under him.

The two went at it for several minutes, fighting to gain the upper hand, until Thom finally gave in. He may have had the swift, athletic edge but Cal clearly held the power with thick, powerful muscles. Even suited up in his impeccably tailored tuxedo, he was able to control the situation. Granted, he would need a tailor to fix the one or two buttons Thom managed to rip off in their scuffle, but overall he remained mostly dapper.

Holding the player in his place, sprawled out and facedown upon the tile floor Cal allowed a few minutes to pass before he spoke again. He was beginning to enjoy the feel of his body pressed against the naked form of the athlete, even if they weren't skin to skin.

"Now," he began, "I'm going to get up."

Thom bucked a bit in his hold.

"And you," Cal calmly continued, "are going to play nice. Because if you don't I'm going to have to resort to a bit of blackmail, which I was hoping I wouldn't have to do."

"What the hell are you talking about?" the player spat.

"Well, Thom, did I not just say that my brother is an officer of the law?"

"Yeah. So?"

"Well, let's just say I have access to several unfavorable files with your name printed on them," Cal threatened. "Imagine that."

"You mother fucker," Thom cursed, before he began to wildly thrash about. "You fuckin' piece of shit!"

Once again, the two men wrestled, with each one fighting for the top position. Again, Cal won the upper hand. However, by the time he gained this advantage, he found himself straddling Thom, face-to-face, with the player's arms extended and pinned against the tile floor.

"Stop," Cal commanded, as he adjusted his suited ass, which was firmly resting upon Thom's throbbing manhood.

"Fuck you," the ball player spat, sending a wad of spit along with the curse, which landed on the satin lapel of Cal's tuxedo jacket.

"Nice. Real civilized of you," Cal simply replied, as he watched the spittle run down the shiny fabric.

"What the hell do you want with me?" Thom bellowed now, still thrashing below Cal.

"I think it's pretty clear."

"Is it?" the player snarled, bucking his hips up, forcing his throbbing tool against his tuxedo-clad assailant's ass, which afforded him the opportunity to leave a smear of pre-cum upon the smooth, dark fabric.

Without replying, Cal leaned in closer. Thom, clearly still confused by the man's intentions, shifted a bit. As Cal came in even closer, their faces mere inches apart, Thom spat once again. Pausing only to lap up the generous wad, Cal continued on his path, forcing his lips upon those of the player.

Thom, thrashing about wildly, made every attempt to break free; yet, Cal managed to match his every move. He also managed to remain lip locked for a good part of the time, quickly forcing his hot tongue between Thom's tightly pursed lips when he could.

The two fought for sometime, each looking for a different resolution to the battle. Cal was eager to claim his prize in its entirety, while Thom aggressively sought his freedom. They each had their strengths, one his agility and the other his brute force; however, once again, might overpowered quickness. Soon enough, Thom found himself bound, with his very jockstrap, to the wooden bench that ran the length of the room.

Laid out, on his back, with his hands bound over his head, the player swiftly realized that he had lost this particular battle. It showed in his body language and his expression.

Cal, standing over his prize now, took a moment to fuss with his once pristine attire. During their match, he had gradually become disheveled, but with a quick tuck here and a simple flick there, he was once again presentable.

"Now, as you can see, T.J., I have gained the upper hand," Cal began, as he walked the length of the player's body, running a finger along his smooth, exposed flesh. "It would be in your best interest to behave and play along."

"Fuck you," Thom muttered defiantly.

"Very well. If that's what you want."

Bringing a hand to the clasp of his tuxedo trousers, Cal slowly undid them, allowing them to slide down his thick legs and pool at his feet. By doing this, he immediately exposed the worn, slightly yellowed jockstrap he was wearing within.

"Look familiar?" Cal questioned the player, after stepping out of his pants and moving closer for Thom to get a better view.

"You sick bastard," Thom spat with a look of disgust on his face.

"Well, come now, you didn't honestly think this was my first time in here. Did you?" Cal replied with a mischievous smile. "I've been a fan for years."

Stepping over the bench, Cal moved into place over Thom, positioning himself above the players still erect cock. With a single finger, he relocated the strap that was hiding his tight, pink pucker, so that his hungry ass could easily take the throbbing bat below. Slowly, inch-by-inch, he proceeded to work the raw rod in. Looking down upon Thom, Cal watched as his handsome face shifted from a look of disgust, to one of surprise, to, finally, utter pleasure.

"NO!" Cal barked. "That's not how we're playing this. You're supposed to be fighting me!"

"Screw you," Thom spat with a huge smile upon his lips. "I'm not going to give you the satisfaction."

Enraged, Cal thrust his tight ass down upon Thom's shaft, devouring the flesh from tip to base. Reaching out, he took the player's exposed nipples between his fingers and began violently twisting them.

"FUCK!" Thom bellowed, thrashing under his assailant.

Cal continued to wildly dance upon the throbbing monster within him. He could feel it sliding in and out of his now moist hole, growing with each thrust, swiftly approaching the moment of climax.

"I want your seed. Oh, fuck, do I want your seed," Cal sang between thrusts, as his muscular ass milked Thom's manhood.

Thom, unable to control his body, as he had wanted to, began to thrust his narrow hips up, causing his cock to drill even deeper into Cal's ass. With each plunge, the player drove the man wild, causing him to grunt and moan as an animal would.

"FUCK!" Cal yelled, as his hands flew once more to Thom's nips.

"SHIT!" Thom barked, as his body tensed under the intense pressure that was being applied to his already sore pecs.

Cal, feeling his body grow slick inside his crisp, white dress shirt, swiftly decided to remedy the build-up of heat by splaying the garment open. With one hand still working the player's nip, his other hand violently tugged at the perfectly tied bow at his neck. The diamond studs that run down the front of his shirt were quick to follow.

"Oh man...," Thom moaned, as his eyes flashed over Cal's sculpted chest and tight abs. And in that moment, the image of the man's slick flesh was enough to trigger a reaction in his loins.

Jet after jet of hot seed was soon splashing along the inside of Cal's ass. The massive load painted the walls of his anus to the edge, spilling out and onto Thom's tight balls and ripped thighs.

"Oh man," Cal parroted, as he too began to erupt inside of his soiled jock.

Gout after gout of creamy, white seed filled the mesh pouch until it began to ooze through the thin material, dripping and smearing onto Thom's taunt abs.

With a satisfied smile, Cal slid off Thom.

"Phew," he exclaimed, as he began to fuss with his attire for the second time since he entered the locker room. "That was hot."

"Yeah," Thom chuckled. "It certainly was."

"So, I'll see you at home later?"

"Yeah, I just have to make my rounds upstairs. You know, schmooze with all the big wigs. Clearly, I've taken a bit too long with my post-game shower," Thom informed Cal, as he stirred in his bindings.

"Ah, been there, done that. I'm finished with this place for the evening, which is a good thing, because I'm not sure I can get myself back to looking even half way presentable," Cal noted, as he attempted to create a perfect bow with his slightly damp tie.

"Well, I guess it's a good thing your father owns not only the team, but the stadium too," Thom casually noted, from his prone position, as he watched his lover slide back into his tailored slacks.

"Yeah. That way I can slip out and not have to hear about it later."

"True."

"Ok, I'm good to go," Cal informed his partner, as he began to make his way toward the exit.

"Uh, aren't you forgetting something?" Thom called, still bound in place.

"Oh. Right," Cal replied, as he quickly stepped back to retrieve his top hat, which sat on the bench not far from Thom. "Thanks," he said, right before he gave him a peck on the cheek. "By the way, next time, I want *you* to play the dominant role. Ever since I was a kid, it's been a fantasy of mine to be roped up in this locker room."

"Perhaps I can get the team to work on you as well," Thom added, as he watched Cal depart.

"Perhaps," Cal replied, as he made his way out.

Thom remained upon the bench, with a smile on his lips, as he thought of this image, until suddenly he remembered he was still bound in place with his jockstrap.

"Cal! Wait!" he called to no avail. "Shit," he cursed. "Just you wait until next time. I'll show you who the fuckin' boss is!" And with that, he continued to thrash in his bindings.

About the Author

Dutch Roberts, born in the seventy-second year of the 1900's, was clearly brought into this world at the very wrong time. Ever since he was a child, he demonstrated signs of being one with the Renaissance. With his interests and hobbies, as well as his talents, as varied as the fantasies in his head, he has always been - and always will be - open to fully exploring whatever opportunities come his way. With the publication of his first book, *Top Hats & Jockstraps*, he is now unflinchingly able to share his dreams and desires with the entire world. Mr. Roberts  currently resides in the heart of New England, poised to take on his next passionate endeavor.

www.ingramcontent.com/pod-product-compliance
Lightning Source LLC
Chambersburg PA
CBHW071227260626
47162CB00004B/1447